Saving Samantha

by

Cindy Causey

Men and Women of Valor

Cover Art by *Teddi Black*

The Wild Rose Press, Inc.
PO Box 708
Adams Basin, NY 14410-0708
Visit us at www.thewildrosepress.com

Publishing History
First Edition, 2025
Trade Paperback ISBN 978-1-5092-6191-8
Digital ISBN 978-1-5092-6192-5

Men and Women of Valor
Published in the United States of America

Dedication

For Traci, Adam, Molly, Erin, and Sarah--my kids, who love me no matter what crazy thing I do next.

Acknowledgments

My journey for Saving Samantha began at DARA, Dallas Area Romance Authors, where guest speakers and writers like Lorraine Heath and Victoria Chancellor inspired me.

During my career at JCPenney, The Legacy Writers Group offered invaluable support and critiques, led by my dear friend Karen Tunnell. Her insightful feedback and unwavering encouragement were and still are crucial to my writing.

My husband Scott read every word of this book, five pages at a time, before bed on Sundays. Sadly, he passed away before it was finished, but I think he would have approved.

More thanks for the love and support of Chris, Gayle, and Diane, my other writers' group, who cheer me on and talk me off the ledge.

I am grateful for the folks at The Wild Rose Press for taking a chance on me again. A special thank you to my editor Judi Mobley, who is smart and knowledgeable and understands my quirkiness.

My friends are the most loyal and wonderful people. They are always interested in my next chapter, literally, and ready to celebrate my small successes. I am so grateful for them and love them all.

And my family. I think they are sometimes surprised that I've done this again. But they are all happy for my books and secretly proud that their mom and sister is a published author.

I'm a little bit proud, too. But I couldn't have done it without the village I have lived in.

Chapter One

Bursting through the surface of the azure water, Samantha Morgan spat out the mouthpiece of her oxygen tank and gasped for a breath of salty sea air. She swam in long, deliberate strokes toward the waiting boat and clambered aboard, feeling more clumsy than usual in the ungainly fins and cumbersome SCUBA gear.

"That was incredible!" she exclaimed, shrugging off the equipment that had been her lifeline for the last hour. "I've never experienced anything like it. I wish we could go back again."

"I'll set us up for tomorrow afternoon, okay?" Jack Stone removed his tank. "Here, let me help you."

He reached over and unbuckled the strap around her waist, letting his hands linger longer than necessary. Her gaze met his.

"I've got it, thanks," Samantha said and turned away. What had she seen in his expression? Fleeting irritation? No matter, the look was gone in an instant.

When they had stowed their gear, the captain of the rented boat started the rumbling engine and headed toward shore.

"Do you come to Key West often?" Samantha asked, plunging her hand into the frigid water of the ice chest to retrieve a beer. She grabbed another and handed it to Jack.

"I haven't been back since I was stationed here in

the Navy. This is where I learned to fly—before Key West became such a tourist Mecca." He popped the top on the beer and took a long draught.

The Keys were as hot as Texas that time of year, Samantha thought, watching a sliver of ice trickle down the side of the can. She was glad to be out of Dallas in September when it was still equator-steamy, but why couldn't her father have picked a cooler place—say Alaska?

Jack leaned back and propped his feet on the cushion next to Samantha. "Is this your first trip to the Keys?"

"Yeah. I'm glad Dad brought the company down for the annual meeting. It's a lot less stuffy than last year in Cincinnati."

"Oh, Cincinnati's not so bad," Jack teased.

Samantha wrinkled her nose at him. "You can't go diving there."

"No, there aren't many oceans in Ohio."

"And no coral reefs like this one. Beautiful, aren't they? It's a shame they're in such jeopardy."

"I don't think the problems with the reefs are as bad as people make out."

"Everyone seems serious about preserving them. You're not even supposed to touch the coral."

"Too bad. I planned to break off a big chunk to put on my mantel."

Samantha stared at him, stunned someone so educated would be ignorant and thoughtless. She began to sputter her objections when he grinned at her. *He's teasing me, the big jerk.*

Then, as if he were pleased with himself for getting her goat, he pulled his sunglasses down from his forehead and over his steel-gray eyes.

"Oh, you think that's funny, eh?" She tossed ice from the cooler onto his bare chest.

He sprung up, gasping. "Okay, okay. Geez, you're a vicious environmentalist!"

Samantha laughed. "Wait until you see what I do when people litter."

When he relaxed against the seat, she studied him from behind her sunglasses. Jack Stone might be more interesting than she had thought, more complicated than the superficial player she'd heard about.

She couldn't help but notice the sheen of water caused his wavy hair to glisten blue/black in the sun. Or the chiseled planes of his face were nearly perfect, except for the tiny crook in his nose, probably the result of a jealous boyfriend's revenge. Or the way the muscles in his long legs bunched and relaxed every time he moved. He was like an exquisite animal, lazing in the sun before he went off to devour a hapless fawn. She smiled at her over-active imagination.

She leaned back, closed her eyes, and let the wind whip her hair dry as the boat cut across the waves, determined not to be one of those fawns.

All she needed was another man who could hurt her with his lies. Especially one like Gary—he was the last in a long line of men who acted like they wanted her but were only after a deep and meaningful relationship with her father, R.L. Morgan, and his money. So, she'd sworn off men for a while. It was a promise she intended to keep. And no amount of Jack Stone charm would make her break it.

Besides, she knew practically nothing about him. He'd only been working at R.L Morgan's direct marketing and internet retail business a little over a month, but long enough for her to hear he had a reputation as a man fond of fast cars and faster women. Other than that, he was a mystery. An irresistible mystery.

And that was the problem, wasn't it? As often as she refused his lunch invitation, he became more charming and persistent. Finally, she succumbed. Lunch seemed innocent enough since they were co-workers in Product Development. So, they enjoyed a couple of meals in the company cafeteria. What could it hurt? It was the polite thing to do; after all, he was a new employee.

Then came the company meeting in Florida.

"What's one dive in the Keys?" she asked herself. He could hardly make a move on her when the boat captain was the chaperone, and they were practically within shouting distance of the company entourage. She'd certainly be able to keep her promise not to get involved with anyone, let alone a wolf in co-worker's clothing like Jack.

So why did she feel unnerved now? The dive was incredible. Jack had been a perfect gentleman. She had enjoyed his company, the repartee, getting to know him, and him getting to know her. It was fun. Too much fun, she thought, frowning to herself. Even as the boat powered through the waves, she knew Jack's magnetism was cutting through her resolve.

When they had docked, pulled T-shirts over their wet suits, and gathered their belongings, Jack stepped off and reached for Samantha's hand. Suddenly, the boat lurched on an incoming wave. She lost her balance and plunged over the side into the yawning gap between the boat and the dock. But before she hit the water, Jack caught her and gently set her down on the old dock's creaking planks.

Samantha gasped. "Thanks."

His arms stayed protectively wrapped around her, his breath close to her ear. "My pleasure. Are you all right?"

"Perfectly fine, thanks." She wriggled out of his grasp, smiling up at him. His mirrored sunglasses made it impossible to read his expression, but she noticed the nearly perfect mouth tightening as she moved away.

Samantha rushed to fill the self-conscious silence that followed and busied herself checking her phone. "I guess we should be going. It's got to be nearly time for the awards banquet."

Gone as quickly as it had come, Jack's disarming smile replaced the hardness in his expression. He glanced at his diver's watch. "Yeah, you're right. It's almost six. Let's get the bikes."

They walked toward the shack, which served as a boat rental shop, and Jack reserved the boat for the following afternoon. She maneuvered her bike from the rack and watched him warily, steeling her resistance.

They walked the bikes through the sand toward the street. "I haven't ridden a bike in years, except the stationary one in the health club," Samantha confessed.

"I think it's great there's a club at the office, but I never have enough time to work out."

"Me either. Since we started working on the winter line, we've stayed late more often than usual."

Jack said, "The boss has been pretty secretive about her ideas."

Samantha pushed a strand of hair out of her face. "I know. She's always been very open. I don't know what's going on."

Jack shrugged. "Maybe it has something to do with the 'altruism' component your dad wants us to incorporate into the new line." He gestured air quotes when he said 'altruism.'

"Possible, but she hasn't told me anything about it. And we need to get moving if we're going to have product by January."

A commotion down the beach grabbed her attention, and she turned to see a small crowd gathering around the next dock. As if of one mind, she and Jack rode their bikes the short distance to take a closer look.

Official Key West vehicles, including several police cars and an ambulance, cluttered the beach. A private fishing boat pulled up to the dock, and two men struggled to hoist a limp, bulky form wrapped in a canvas tarp over the side to waiting paramedics. They carried it down the dock toward the ambulance. One man stumbled and sprawled face down in the sand. The object, torn from his grasp, spilled open; a lifeless body rolled onto the beach—a woman in a tiger-striped swimsuit, bloated from hours in the water.

The crowd gasped and rushed forward, Jack and Samantha among them. Before the paramedics could recover and wrap the body, Samantha screamed.

"Joanna! Joanna!" She lurched forward. "God, no, it's Joanna!"

Jack put his arms around her and pulled her away. Samantha grew more hysterical. "It's Joanna! Help her! She's not breathing, Jack! Help her!"

"Sam, I can't do anything. She's gone." He held her tight as she struggled to reach Joanna. Giving up, she turned away and sobbed against his chest, soaking his shirt.

The paramedics managed to get the body into the ambulance and drove away, sirens clearing a path through the crowd. The police converged on Samantha, still wrapped in Jack's protective embrace.

"Miss, we need to ask you some questions."

Jack spoke before she could answer. "Officer, can this wait? She's clearly too upset now."

"No, I'm afraid it can't. We need to find out what happened to this woman as quickly as possible." He motioned for another man to come forward.

The second man, short and squat, had a bulbous nose and red face. His ill-fitting suit looked as if he'd slept in it. "I'm Detective Jordan," he said, pen poised above a dilapidated notepad. "It's obvious you know the deceased. Could you please tell me who she is?"

Samantha glanced at Jack for support. "Yes," she answered. "Her name is Joanna Levinson." Then, her voice catching in her throat, she added, "She's our boss."

****

The sun had long since gone down on Mallory Square when Jack and Samantha trudged up the steps and into the lobby of the Explorers Hotel.

Samantha stifled a yawn. "I can't believe they kept us there so long." She sank into one of the comfortable lounge chairs gracing the room. "We missed the whole awards banquet."

Jack chose a matching seat next to hers, extending his lean frame to its full length and stretched like a jungle cat. "Small town cops. This is their one big crime for the year. They want to milk it for all it's worth."

"I suppose Dad must know by now."

"I called him while they were talking to you."

She stared silently into the potted palm between

them, then she and Jack jumped to their feet when the unmistakable, booming voice of Robert Lowden Morgan filled the room.

"Sam, is that you?" The huge man came out of the bar and bustled over to where his daughter stood. He brushed a kiss across the top of her head.

"Hello, Mr. Morgan," Jack said, extending his hand to his boss. At six-foot-two, Jack stood eye to eye with the legendary retail giant but only about half as broad.

Close behind R.L. trotted Samantha's mother, Grace, as tiny as R.L. was big. A riot of auburn hair threatened to overpower her pixie face.

R.L. waved Jack back into his seat. "Please, Stone, sit down. I know you're tired." Turning to his daughter, he asked, "Are you all right, Sam?"

"Yes, Dad, I'm perfectly fine. It's a shock, that's all."

Grace grabbed Samantha by the shoulders, scanned her up and down, and pulled her into an embrace that belied the little woman's size. "Are you sure you're okay? My goodness…Joanna…dead." Still holding her daughter, she turned her attention to Jack. "Thank God you were there, Jack. How awful for you both." She reached out a manicured hand and patted his arm.

"We're fine, Mrs. Morgan. But it was a terrible scene."

Released from her mother's arms, Samantha rubbed the back of her hand across her eyes. "I had breakfast with Joanna, and now… Who would do such a thing?" She squeezed her eyes shut against the memory of her boss at the table, the tiger-striped swimsuit peeking out through a black gauze cover-up.

Her dad turned to Jack, who still stood in his boss'

presence. "Are they sure it was murder, then? They wouldn't tell me a damn thing."

"No, sir, they don't know anything yet. Not until after the autopsy, but the coroner on the scene suspected strangulation because of the marks on her throat. Probably by rope or boat line."

Samantha shuddered. "I think I'll go upstairs to my room." She clasped her arms about her, feeling a sudden chill though the lobby was heavy with heat and humidity.

"Have you eaten?" her mother asked, her face clouded by worry.

"No, I'll call room service if I get hungry."

"I'll walk you up," Jack offered.

"That's not necessary." Samantha's nerves were so frayed she didn't know how much longer she could hold on. She wanted only the solitude of her room.

In a voice that implied there would be no discussion, her dad said, "I insist."

Samantha tamped down a flash of anger. She wasn't in the mood for her father's high-handed tactics, but she didn't have the strength to argue. Also, was she mistaken, or had she seen a surreptitious glance pass between Jack and her father?

Jack reasoned, "Look, I've been by your side every step of the way today. A few more won't hurt."

His gentle smile broke through Samantha's resolve. She shrugged and turned toward her parents. "All right, then, goodnight." She kissed her mother's soft cheek, then her father's bristly one.

He smiled at her, then said to Jack, "Come see me in the morning, Stone."

Jack nodded. He took Samantha's elbow lightly and steered her to the elevators. "Goodnight, Mrs.

Morgan…sir," he called back over his shoulder to her parents.

****

"Thanks for everything, Jack," Samantha said when they reached her room and she unlocked the door. "I couldn't have gotten through the day without you." She laid her hand on his arm, aware of the warmth of his skin beneath the dusting of dark hair. He covered her hand with his and looked at her, a trace of concern clouding his expression.

"You're welcome. I'm sorry about Joanna."

"Me, too." She swiped away the tears welling in her eyes. "I don't seem to be able to stop crying." Her whole body slumped in an involuntary sob. Jack scooped her up, carried her through the open door, and set her on the bed.

He sat beside her, holding her until her sobbing quieted, rocking her gently and stroking her hair. At last, she sighed heavily against his chest. She gazed into his unreadable face, his eyes hooded and smoky gray.

"I'm okay now, I think," she murmured, swiping at his shirt. "I keep crying on you. I'm sorry I'm so emotional."

"I think you're rather amazing," Jack said, and somehow, she knew he meant it.

Without warning, he stood, leaving her alone on the bed. "Get some rest. I'll see you at breakfast."

He closed the door behind him and was gone.

What the hell was that all about?

Even in her exhausted and saddened state, Samantha sensed something weird going on. But she couldn't put her finger on it.

****

Jack tossed and turned in bed later, kicking himself mentally for nearly taking advantage of Samantha when she was so emotionally vulnerable. Kissing her would have been lower than he had thought himself capable of behaving.

But that was all he had wanted to do.

It had taken all his willpower to leave her on the bed, eyes swollen from crying, nerves shattered, lips quivering, beautiful…vulnerable.

Sure, he had never been one to turn down the charms of a beautiful woman, especially one who had money and power—or whose father had money and power. But he wasn't in the habit of forcing himself on someone who seemed so intent on keeping herself at arm's length.

What was that about anyway? She seemed to enjoy his company, and they got along great until he tried to touch her. Then she froze like an ice queen.

Of course, he had no business trying to get close to Samantha Morgan. His job description didn't include fraternizing, especially not with R.L.'s daughter.

Six weeks earlier, Vince Samuels, the owner of Bolton's Valor Security and Investigations, had called him into their Colorado office and made that crystal clear.

"Look, Jack, I like you, you know I do, but you're on my last nerve," he had thundered. "If I get one more report about your amorous habits around the clients, it'll be your last job for me. And that includes their wives, daughters, sisters, exes, or even their mothers! No exceptions. Got it?"

Jack had gotten it. It wasn't the first time he'd been taken to task by Vince or his lovely partner, the buff and beautiful Jacy McClain. But it would be the last. He would not be getting involved on the job again, no matter how irresistible his client might be. "I swear, Vince, no more women. I've learned my lesson. Besides, I don't much like women complaining about me."

Vince chuckled. "It's not the women who have been complaining, Jack."

Jack studied his feet. "Oh…sorry."

"Never mind. I'm sending you to Texas, as far away from Colorado as possible. A company there has been getting vague, anonymous threats. It's all in here." Vince handed him a file folder. "Find out where they're coming from and keep an eye on the employees. It could be an inside job. You'll report directly to R.L. Morgan."

Jack nodded. "No problem."

Vince scowled. "And no women."

"Aye, sir," Jack had said with a mock salute and packed his bags for Texas.

It didn't take long for things to go ass upward.

Jack remembered the first time he met Samantha Morgan. He was coming out of R.L.'s office the first day and ran headlong into her, scattering papers everywhere. R.L. introduced her as the 'up-and-coming leader in direct marketing.'

The introduction wasn't necessary since he'd seen her in the file Vince gave him and had memorized everything about her, including her vital statistics.

"Dad." She blushed, then extended her hand. "Hello, I'm Samantha Morgan."

Jack remembered her hand, soft and warm. And he noticed her fingernails were not the fancy painted claws many women sported these days. They were shiny and short.

When he looked into her face, her smile went clear

to her eyes. And those eyes! Emerald-green and huge, ringed in heavy, dark lashes. They were wide open and accepting, not shrewd and calculating. They were innocent, incredible eyes.

Everything about Samantha Morgan seemed fresh and new. Her clear, olive-hued complexion, unspoiled by heavy makeup, and free-flowing, auburn hair, thick and shiny, not lacquered in place, left Jack with the impression she was genuine.

Not his type at all.

It should be easy to keep his distance.

But he found himself working close to Samantha and her boss, Joanna Levinson, in Product Development. The threats had been sent to the department, but only Joanna was aware of them. R.L. made no bones about the fact Jack was not only to find the source of the threats but also protect Joanna and especially his daughter.

Only Joanna would know about any potential danger. And since the threats might be coming from inside the company, Jack's real identity would be kept secret from everyone except her and R.L.

Since then, he had spent time with Joanna, discussing the threats and possible enemies or motives. But they had managed to keep Samantha in the dark. He had invited Samantha to lunch a couple of times, on the pretense of getting to know her, but it was clear she knew nothing about the threats or who might be behind them.

The SCUBA diving in the Keys was a way to stay close and keep an eye on her. Although he had to admit, keeping things strictly business between himself and the lovely Miss Morgan had been hard.

He had originally asked Joanna if she wanted to go diving to keep an eye on *her*, but she had begged off, saying she had to do prep work for a meeting. And then she turned up on the beach…dead.

If he had been with Joanna instead of Samantha, could he have saved her? Or would it have been Samantha's body on the beach? The thought upset him more than he would have thought possible.

Staring at the ceiling, Jack could still feel Sam in his arms, luscious and warm, snuggled up next to him. Keeping his distance from her would be one of the hardest things he'd ever done.

Chapter Two

Samantha awoke to a clear, bright day. A cool breeze wafted through the royal poinciana trees. Her eyes were red-rimmed and swollen when she put on her makeup. The ivory linen pants and soft pink tank she chose only added to the paleness of her reflection in the mirror. Somehow, she didn't care.

She joined her co-workers for breakfast on the terrace, taking a seat at her parents' table. In his usual commanding style, her dad had arranged for his employees to be served away from the prying eyes of the other guests in the hotel. Most planned to go home later in the day, their meetings and recreation cut short by the death of one of their colleagues. They sipped coffee, munched on pastries, and whispered among themselves. Samantha picked at her food and tried to ignore their furtive glances.

The distinctive sound of a text message on her phone caught her off guard. Detective Jordan wanted to see her at the station at ten a.m. She showed the message to her father. He responded as she expected.

"I'll be damned if I'm going to let you spend another day at the station. Who does this Jordan think he is, anyway? We'll see about this," he bellowed, rattling the coffee cups on the table.

Grace tried to soothe him, urging him to lower his voice.

"It's all right, Dad," Samantha said. "I don't mind. I'll do anything to help them solve Joanna's murder."

"What else could they possibly ask you? "

"Dad, they're just doing their jobs. I'd like to cooperate if I can."

"Well, you can't go alone. Someone has to go with you," he conceded, apparently unable to maintain his steely tone toward his beloved daughter.

A familiar voice came from across the terrace, "I'll go." Jack, dressed in perfectly creased khaki trousers and a navy polo shirt clinging to his sculpted chest, crossed to where she sat. "That is if Samantha doesn't mind."

She didn't want Jack to come. She had spent the better part of the night alternately crying over Joanna's death and feeling confused about Jack's abrupt departure.

She scowled. "Didn't you get enough of Jordan's third-degree yesterday? Please don't feel obligated to spend what's left of your time here in a police station. Surely, there must be something you'd rather do."

She was awash in conflicting emotions about Jack. She could still feel the warmth of his embrace and how gentle he had been with her. Gary had never been gentle. No one else had, either, for that matter. The prospect of spending the day in the company of Jack Stone was dangerous at best.

Jack argued, "I've seen everything there is to see here already. Besides, Detective Jordan summoned me to his office, also. And, as I understand it, he'll want to speak to everyone who knew Joanna."

Another messenger approached the table, interrupting R.L. Morgan's convulsive protests. The trembling waiter handed him a hotel phone.

Her dad's thundering confirmed it was Jordan on the phone. But his arguments fell on deaf ears because he nodded his head after a few moments, said he would see to it, and punched the phone off.

"Met your match, eh, Dad?" Samantha teased.

"I always want to cooperate with the authorities," R.L. growled and resumed attacking his breakfast.

"Now, as far as having an escort to the station," Samantha said, squaring her shoulders and thrusting out her chin in defiance. "I'm perfectly capable of looking out for myself, although you two don't seem to think so."

Her dad steamrolled ahead. "Thanks for taking her, Stone. I have my hands full here. Joanna's family is coming in to claim the body, and we're still going to try to have a board meeting this morning."

"Well, if you two gentlemen are finished planning my day for me, I think I'll get ready to leave." Samantha tossed an overly dramatic glare at Jack and her father, blew a kiss to her mother, and went into the hotel.

****

"Why is she all riled up?" R.L. asked his wife when Samantha had gone.

Grace chuckled. "Your daughter is an independent woman, honey. I imagine she feels a little overprotected at the moment."

R.L. cut his eyes to Jack. "All the same, Stone, I'll feel better if you're there."

"Yes, sir, I won't let her out of my sight," Jack promised. A picture of Samantha flashed into his mind: sleek body, shining hair, and gemstone eyes that seemed too green for their own good. Watching her wouldn't be such a bad way to spend the day.

And after his meeting with R.L. earlier that morning,

it was now the main focus of his job for Bolton.

"Look here, Stone," the big man had blustered when they met on the terrace over coffee. "This is a terrible business about Joanna. Murder, my God! And right under your nose. What am I paying you for, anyway?"

"We had no way of knowing things would escalate in such a way, sir. The threats didn't target Joanna specifically."

"Well, you better stay near my daughter night and day. You've got to keep her safe and get to the bottom of this."

"Yes, sir, of course. Samantha's safety will be my priority."

"But she can't know anything about it. Not a thing."

"Under the circumstances, it might be better if she did, sir."

"No, she won't have it. Too independent. You have to keep an eye on her."

Jack knew Samantha wouldn't make it easy. "Yes, of course. I understand." He had left then to call Vince and update him on the turn his assignment had taken. He needed his boss to know getting close to Samantha was not his idea. Not his idea at all.

Vince had not been pleased. "Oh, great. Now he's put the fox in the henhouse. Exactly what I was trying to avoid."

"I know. I know. But look, I'll behave. She's going to hate me anyway since I have to practically stalk her to keep her safe."

"Good," Vince said. "Let her hate you. Find out who's sending the messages and who killed that poor woman. Then get the hell out of there."

"Right. That's my plan."

Vince groaned, then clicked off the phone. He apparently had no faith Jack could pull it off without a romantic entanglement.

Jack grimaced. *I'm not sure I can pull it off either.*

Samantha rounded the corner of the hotel lobby. Her hair shone copper in the light streaming in from the terrace doors.

A grim determination marked her lovely features, and Jack couldn't help but notice the scowl she cast in his direction. He forced a smile and swept the ground in an exaggerated bow. "At your service."

"I love this," she said, her voice dripping in sarcasm. "Thirty-two years old, and my father thinks I need a chaperone." She brushed past him. "Well, come on. Let's get this over with."

Great idea.

****

Once inside the station, she and Jack were escorted to a room where several officers from the beach, including Detective Jordan, were seated.

Jordan flipped open his notepad. "Miss Morgan, Mr. Stone. We're sorry to have brought you in again so soon, but we understand you're leaving, and we need more information if we're going to discover who killed Miss Levinson."

"Then you're sure it was murder?" Jack asked.

"Yes, we are. Further examination of the body proved it."

Samantha shuddered, and Jack put an arm around her shoulder.

"Take a seat, please." The detective leafed through the notepad and then looked at Samantha.

"Miss Morgan, what do you know about Miss

19

Levinson's personal life?"

"Her personal life? Not much. No husband, no children. She went home to New Hampshire occasionally to see her parents. She mentioned she was dating someone there, but I don't know who he was. I don't think she had been seeing him for very long. Only a few weeks."

"How closely did you work with her? Were you working on any projects together?"

"We worked together constantly." Samantha paused, thinking about how she and Joanna had worked so well together, laughing often and sharing the same ideas and values. Although Samantha was a few years younger, she had always thought of her boss as more of a co-worker than a supervisor. She shook the memories away. There would be time for grieving later.

"We were in the process of building next year's winter line. Looking for new products, different fabrics, new color palettes."

"Anything unusual—different from previous seasons?"

Samantha smiled a little. "I hope almost everything is different, Detective Jordan. We can't do much business selling last year's merchandise. But if you mean anything completely different…" She ran one fingertip over her lips, thinking. "There was one project." She looked at Jack and said, "The 'altruism' component."

Jack turned to Jordan. "Right. We were instructed to find a product that was beneficial in some way."

Detective Jordan cocked his head. "Beneficial?"

Samantha explained, "Something that would help the environment or include a donation to a worthwhile cause. We settled on clothing made from recycled water bottles."

Jordan's head jerked up. "Hmm…so these would have been companies unfamiliar to you?"

"Yes, that's right," Samantha answered.

"I'll need the specifics for them. Names, locations." Detective Jordan scribbled furiously.

Jack shook his head. "I'm afraid we can't help you. Joanna hadn't shared any information. Maybe she wasn't far enough along in her research."

"Do you think there would be information in her files in Dallas?"

Samantha replied, "I would think so."

Jack leaned forward. "What are you thinking, detective? That her death is related to our business? Like industrial espionage or fraud?"

"Well, until we know more about Miss Levinson, we can't ignore any lead," Jordan said. "When you get back to Dallas, I'll have the police secure her office, but would you please study your boss' files for any possible piece of information that might help us?"

Samantha was stunned. "You don't think she was killed because of work, do you? You can't be serious!"

"Like I said, Miss Morgan, we can't ignore any lead. I imagine Miss Levinson died at the hands of a stranger in a perfectly random act of violence. Still, until the autopsy is complete, and the investigation concluded, we can't be sure."

Jordan turned his attention to Jack. "How well did you know Miss Levinson?"

"Not well," Jack answered, leaning back in his chair. "We worked together every day, but I've only been at the company a little over a month. We went to lunch a few times."

"Oh, in what capacity?" Jordan asked.

"I wanted to get to know her better. You know, schmooze the boss."

Jordan chuckled. "Sure, but nothing more?"

"There was one dinner."

"You two went to dinner?" Samantha asked, surprised. She hadn't been aware they had gone out to dinner. Lunches, yes. To get acquainted, sure. But dinner seemed…so…intimate.

Jack shifted in his chair. "Yes, one dinner. To talk about business."

"Mm-hmm." Samantha didn't buy that for a minute.

The detective asked several more questions, but Samantha didn't hear the answers. Jack was a player, and he was probably playing her.

He had gone out with Joanna—probably slept with her, given his reputation—but neither one had ever mentioned it. Why? There were no rules at R.L. Morgan about dating a co-worker. So, Jack must have been using her to get his foot in the door at the company. He probably had big plans to climb the corporate ladder.

Which is, of course, where I come in. Get close to the boss' daughter. Get a rung up on the corporate ladder, for sure. How could I have been so stupid? I've seen it all before.

Her decision not to get involved with Jack Stone suddenly became wrapped in metaphorical steel bands.

Detective Jordan flipped the notepad shut and returned the pen to his shirt pocket.

"Thank you for your cooperation. If you find anything in the files, please call me." He handed them his card. "We'll have the autopsy results this afternoon and will release the body to the next of kin. I believe they're arriving today. After we talk to the rest of the employees, everyone will be free to leave."

He shook Jack's hand, then took Samantha's in his. "I'm sorry about your boss, Miss Morgan. And I'm sorry your visit to Key West was marred in such a terrible way. I hope you'll come back again someday when you can fully enjoy the beauty and serenity of our island." The detective smiled sincerely.

"Thank you," she said, thoroughly miserable. "I hope so, too."

****

The distinctive ring of her cell phone shattered the deep sleep Samantha had at last found. It was mid-afternoon, and the sun slipping through the closed shades painted eerie patterns on the washed-wood floor. Groggy and disoriented, she grabbed the phone to cease its rude ringing.

"Hello," she muttered.

"Sam, it's Jack." He paused.

She didn't answer.

He plunged forward. "I thought we could go for a drink. There's an unusual place I know, close to Mallory Square. We could watch the sunset and then have dinner somewhere. I thought you might want to see more of the island before we leave tomorrow."

"Jack, I'm not up to it," she replied, trying to sound as uninterested as possible.

"Look, Sam." What was it Samantha thought she heard in his voice? Sincerity? From the man who was lying to her about his motives?

"We need to talk. I need to explain to you about me and Joanna."

"Jack, you don't owe me any explanation," she lied.

"You're free to take anyone you wish to dinner."

"I wish to take *you* to dinner—in thirty minutes. No arguments. I'll meet you in the lobby."

The phone clicked off.

What an arrogant jerk! Samantha fumed, tossing the phone aside. If he thought he could order her around, he was crazy. She would not meet him in the lobby or anywhere else!

Pacing the room, Samantha forced herself to calm down. She opened the balcony doors and went out to watch the little island as it prepared for the evening. The sun was low in the sky and soon would disappear off the edge of Mallory Square, providing the setting for the nightly ritual of music, fun, and frolic in a carnival atmosphere that had come to epitomize life on Key West. Samantha had looked forward to experiencing it on this trip but had yet to be a part of it.

"I will not let Joanna or Jack ruin every single thing about this trip," she said out loud, stamping her foot. She could go to the sunset celebration alone. She certainly didn't need Jack Stone to take her.

Tearing through her clothes to find something fun to wear, Samantha tingled with energy. It felt good after the pall of the last two days. Then, suddenly, she stopped. Jack wouldn't wait patiently if she didn't show up in the lobby. He would come to her room, and being a Neanderthal, he would probably drag her out by her hair.

But not if she weren't there.

She shrugged into a colorful sundress and glanced at herself in the mirror. Her shoulders were bronzed from the sun, and her eyes glowed in anticipation. She gathered her hair in a big clip and let a few wisps loosely frame her face, then smiled at her reflection.

I'll have to sneak out.

****

She saw him immediately from her hiding place behind the potted palm, and her heart skipped a beat. Jack stood talking to one of the company's buyers, laughing casually. His knit shirt was the perfect foil for his well-defined chest and broad shoulders, and Samantha slightly regretted she wouldn't be on his arm for the evening.

She backed out of the lobby and left the hotel through the terrace door next to the parking lot. She turned onto one of the side roads leading directly to Mallory Square.

A few minutes later, she reached the square and paused to get her bearings, deciding where she might have dinner. She heard Jack's voice behind her.

"I'm hoping you got confused and thought I said to meet me here."

When she spun around, he continued, "I'd hate to think you were going to stand me up. That would be so rude."

Samantha squared her shoulders. "Jack, you hung up before I could tell you I couldn't go out with you tonight."

"Oh, you have other plans?" he asked, a frown furrowing his brow.

"Not especially. I wanted to be alone. You understand," she finished brightly and tossed her head to signal the end of the conversation.

"No, I don't understand," Jack said between clenched teeth, his patience apparently waning. "I don't understand a helluva lot, but I wanted you to come to dinner so we could straighten out what *you* don't understand!"

Samantha didn't understand any of that but took a step closer to Jack. She lowered her voice, practically spitting out the words as she glared at him through narrowed eyes. "Look, Jack, there's nothing to straighten out. You dated Joanna. Now I'm next in line. This is your modus operandi. I've seen it all before."

She paused, then raised her voice to a normal level and said as sarcastically as possible, "Maybe you plan to seduce everyone at R.L. Morgan and seize control of the company. I should probably warn Bobbie." She paused again, registering the steel-hard expression on Jack's face, the healthy tan replaced by a kind of concrete grayness. Throwing their sixty-year-old admin into the mix was probably uncalled for, so she softened her attack. "It doesn't matter, Jack. Let's forget the whole thing. We have to work together. We can keep things business casual."

She turned on her heel, but he said in a voice that made her stop. "Sam, wait." She turned around. "Please, it's important we talk, especially since we have to work together." She stood rooted to the spot, motivated now by curiosity.

Why does it matter so much to him?

"Okay, then," she sighed.

"Good, come on." He grabbed her hand and led her across the square.

Samantha harrumphed in feigned disgust, for try as she might—and she was mightily trying—she couldn't stay mad at Jack. Perhaps it was his hand clutching hers so tight she thought her fingers might break or the unexplainable chemistry between them, but it was a powerful force that threatened her promise to keep her distance from him.

Especially when he seemed so sincere.

Struggling to stay aloof, Samantha barely noticed he had turned off Duval Street and she was now in front of the Purple Finch, a Key West landmark and favorite of the locals, according to Jack, who recited its attributes to her.

"They have great drinks and terrible art here," he said, maneuvering them to a small table close to the bar. "And on any given night, you never know what kind of music will be on tap. Anything from live blues to classic rock. I've even been here on a Sunday when someone read poetry."

No one was reading poetry tonight, Samantha noticed. The open-air bar sported pool tables and reggae music. Jack ordered two tall, cool tropical drinks with names Samantha didn't recognize. Then, they settled in to watch people passing by.

"When we finish, we can go to Mallory Square and see the sunset. It's quite a celebration. You've heard about it, I'm sure," Jack said as their drinks, resplendent with fresh fruit bobbing on top, were placed in front of them.

"Of course. It's one of the things I wanted to do while I was here," Samantha answered and sipped the delicious concoction, tasting the hefty portion of rum. "But that's not why we're here, is it, Jack? Why don't you tell me what you wanted to talk about?"

"You're certainly to the point, aren't you? A little like your father."

"What the hell does that mean?" she snapped.

He raised his hands in surrender. "I mean, you're very direct. Not much small talk." He paused. "I want to talk to you about me and Joanna."

She clenched her hands in her lap and studied them as if they belonged to someone else.

Why am I so bothered? Jack is nothing to me.

"What is there to know?" she said. "You were in a relationship with Joanna. I can't imagine why you would keep it a secret."

Jack raised his voice the slightest bit. "Look, there was no relationship. I took her to lunch a few times and to dinner once. That's all there was to it. I was simply trying to get to know her better, you know, get a lay of the land, sort of, for my new job. It was never going to be any more than that."

Samantha stared at him. "Why not? Joanna was warm and funny and intelligent…and very pretty." She stared back into her lap, her eyes misting at the memory of her boss.

"She was all those things," Jack said, his voice gentler. "But she was also in love with someone else, like you told Jordan."

Samantha jerked her head up to meet Jack's level gaze. Her heart skipped a beat. "She told you about the man in New Hampshire?"

"Yes, the night we were at dinner. She seemed completely into the guy."

He was telling the truth. I was wrong. She took a long sip of her drink, feeling its icy warmth travel through her.

Jack went on, "She never said who it was or anything about him. It was all very hush-hush."

Samantha shook her head. "Poor man! How will he ever know what's happened to her?"

"I'm sure the authorities in Dallas will find him. Or

maybe her family knows who he is. At any rate, it's out of our hands now."

"Maybe there'll be something about him in her office," Samantha suggested.

"Maybe." Jack drained his drink. "We'd better go if we're going to see the sunset." He led her out of the bar and into the reddening sky.

****

A riot of sights and sounds assaulted Samantha and Jack as they approached Mallory Square. Sword-swallowers, flame-tossing jugglers, and a cacophony of street musicians vied for their attention while food vendors hawked everything from conch fritters to tropical fruit salad. Gawking tourists, taking pictures on their cell phones, snagged hand-painted T-shirts, shell jewelry, and other island specialties. All were present to watch the nightly sunset ritual—nature's breathtaking finale to a glorious day on Key West.

The carnival atmosphere captivated Samantha. She and Jack stopped to watch a one-man band, his arms and legs banging away on an array of cymbals and drums while he alternately blew into a whistle and harmonica. Jack tossed a couple of bills into the hat at the man's feet, and they moved on to sample a refreshing Key Limeade.

When the sun began its slow descent, painting the sky around it and the water below in a palette of vivid colors, Jack's hand brushed against hers, and she found herself wanting to lace her fingers through his. She glanced up to see him watching her, his smoky eyes penetrating, searching. She thought he might kiss her.

But they were jostled by a group of rowdy tourists, and the moment was gone.

****

He had nearly kissed her.

Again. Then, before he lost his mind completely, drowning in those eyes of hers, he came to his senses and took her to dinner instead. Thank God for the drunk tourists. After dinner, she and Jack returned to the hotel, and he offered a lame excuse to keep from walking her to her room.

He sensed her confusion, but something else, too. Relief? Whatever. He was relieved himself.

It was bad enough he had lied to her. He had to get his relationship with Samantha back on an even keel if he were ever going to stay close enough to protect her. So, he reinforced the lie he told Jordan about getting to know Joanna better. The truth was he had taken Joanna to dinner so they could talk about the threats away from the office and nosy co-workers like the ever-present Bobbie, whose favorite pastime was coffee bar gossip.

Hopefully, Samantha would never find out about the threats, who he was, or why he was there. Her trust in him was tenuous at best. The truth would shatter it for sure.

If he could resist these temptations as they presented themselves and lie to Sam as little as possible, he could keep his promise to Vince, keep Sam safe, and keep his job.

One day at a time, Stone. One day at a time.

****

"This is impossible!" Samantha exclaimed. Since returning to work on Monday, she and Jack had rarely left the unoccupied cubicle that had been Joanna's office but hadn't found anything of interest.

The Dallas police had come in, dusted for prints, collected a few odds and ends, but seemed uninterested in a crime occurring outside their jurisdiction. They had cleared out after a few hours, leaving Jack and Joanna free to rifle through files to their heart's content.

Samantha tossed a folder onto the cluttered desk. "Three days of combing through everything, and I can't find a thing even slightly out of the ordinary. Detective Jordan must have been wrong to think Joanna's murder had anything to do with R.L. Morgan."

Jack put another folder on the stack going to his office later. "Look, take a break. I'm going to go for coffee. Back in a minute."

Samantha collapsed into the desk chair, happy for a moment alone.

Her forced proximity to Jack was unnerving. The tiny cubicle afforded little breathing room, and she constantly bumped into him or had to shuffle positions carrying files from Joanna's office to her own. Bobbie was also in the mix, providing coffee, labels, filing services, and moral support. Samantha was grateful and put on a happy face for everyone, including Jack.

It was bad enough no one talked of anything but Joanna's death and how Jack and Samantha had seen her—poor thing, and how awful that must have been, and did she want to talk about it? No, she did not want to talk about it. She didn't want to think about it, yet here she was in Joanna's office, packing up her coffee mug and the scarf she wore all the time.

At least if I'm thinking about Joanna, I can't think about Jack.

Thinking about Jack was disastrous. Just as the last night in Key West had been. Even though Samantha had been the one to put a stop to any future relationship between her and Jack, she was now somehow dissatisfied and uneasy.

She had what she wanted, didn't she? No more men to cause her the misery and stress Gary and the others had. So why did she feel so rotten? She told herself it was because of Joanna's death, but still, she couldn't shake the feeling. And she couldn't shake Jack.

He was there every minute of the day, either in Joanna's cubicle with Samantha, in a meeting with Samantha, or in conversation with Samantha about work. She needed a break from Jack. Somewhere he wasn't.

When he returned carrying the coffee, she thanked him, took a bundle of files next door to her office, and settled in to read through them. He did the same.

He's probably happy to be away from me, too.

Her files were from the altruism project Joanna had been working on. She had amassed considerable research on different manufacturers, distinguishing each by a color-coded file folder. She and Joanna had gone through several together and had rejected them for various reasons. Samantha recited them to herself as she tossed each aside—too expensive, couldn't deliver on time, the wrong type of merchandise, or poor quality.

Three folders she had never seen before remained: a yellow one labeled Eco-Tek, located around the corner in Frisco, Texas; a blue one labeled Green Earth Enterprises, a company in Meredith, New Hampshire; and a green one labeled Bottle Stoppers, out of St. Louis.

"Cute name." She called out to Jack, "Come over here for a second. You should see these."

He came in and sat down. "What's up?"

"Look at this." She handed him the blue folder.

He opened it and scanned the first page. "New Hampshire, huh? Interesting. We need to let them know about Joanna and re-establish contact, don't you think?"

"Right, and see if we can get a handle on who Joanna was dating. Maybe it was someone from the company." She took the folder back and handed him the green one. "What about this?"

"Bottle Stoppers. Clever name."

"I agree." She took the folder and gave him back the one for Green Earth. "You take that one, and I'll look into…" She picked up the yellow folder. "Eco-Tek."

"Okay, let's circle back tomorrow on these two, and then we'll take on Bottle Stoppers."

"Perfect."

Jack left her cubicle, blue folder in hand. Samantha flipped through the yellow one until she found the name of the President, Steed Lambert. "Cool name," she thought as she dialed the phone and said it aloud to the person who answered.

The secretary who intercepted the call seemed confused to hear from someone at R.L. Morgan other than Joanna. Still, when Samantha explained about her boss' untimely death, the woman quickly set up an appointment with Mr. Lambert for the following day.

Samantha hung up the phone and glanced at her watch. She had enough time to get to the church for Joanna's memorial service.

****

R.L. Morgan employees packed the tiny church in Frisco. Many worked directly with Joanna and Samantha, but folks from the entire company lined the pews, wanting to show their respect and also take the afternoon off work.

Samantha nodded to Joe Gibson, the head of her division and Joanna's boss. Then she took a seat next to her mother and father at the front of the church. Jack, she noticed, sat amid other co-workers toward the back.

Since the family had already taken the body back to New Hampshire for burial, there was no casket at the front of the church, a fact for which Samantha was grateful. She had yet to get over the shock of seeing Joanna's body hurled onto the sand, and she doubted she could think of her lying serenely in a coffin without losing her composure completely.

The service was brief. Samantha thought everyone seemed more stunned than anything else. It was one thing to have a co-worker die; it was quite another to have her murdered on a business trip. She shuddered at the thought that someone sitting in the service might be the murderer. Surely no one she knew could do such a horrible thing.

As she left the church, Joe Gibson waved her down.

"Samantha, would you come by my office in the morning, about ten? There's something I'd like to talk to you about."

"Certainly," she replied, puzzled but trying not to show it. She'd never been summoned to the Divisional Manager's office before.

"Fine, I'll see you then," he said and moved to speak to her mother and father.

She stood on the steps, chewing on her bottom lip. *What could he want?*

"What did you think about the service?" Jack said from behind her, startling her out of her reverie.

"I thought it was nice." She turned and looked at his sculpted features, black hair glistening in the afternoon sun and the omnipresent mirrored glasses shading his eyes. She had never seen him in a suit, but the black one he wore fit him like a glove.

A smile played at the corner of his mouth. "Yeah, it was exactly right." He paused. "I called Green Earth. They'll get back to me about a meeting. I guess we'll have to go up there eventually."

Samantha nodded. "I have a meeting with Steed Lambert at Eco-Tek tomorrow. "

"Interesting name." Jack frowned.

"Yeah, I thought so."

"Maybe we'll find out something about Joanna's death from one of them."

Samantha shook her head. "I don't know. We haven't found a single thing in her office or her files that looks suspicious. I think Detective Jordan is barking up the wrong tree."

"Probably." Another pause.

Samantha searched for something to say.

Without warning, Jack reached up and brushed a strand of hair from her cheek. His touch was feather-light, yet a spark of electricity made her jump. Her hand flew to her face.

His mouth hardened into a thin line. "Sorry, I didn't mean to scare you. I won't bite, you know." He turned and walked briskly to his car, leaving her alone on the steps.

****

Samantha left her office the next morning, rounded the corner and walked the twenty feet to Joe Gibson's office, a cubicle double the size of hers. She shook hands with him and took the seat he motioned to.

He got right to the point. "We want you to take Joanna's job as head of Product Development." He paused long enough for her to digest his statement.

"You've been working closely for several years, and we feel you're ready for this promotion. We're sorry the circumstances came about as they did, but we're glad someone as qualified as you can step in and take over immediately. The change will be effective the first of the month."

"Well," Samantha let out a breath. "This is unexpected, although I suppose someone has to take Joanna's position. I hadn't thought about it, I guess." She straightened her shoulders. "I'm thrilled, of course, and thank you for the vote of confidence."

Joe stood and reached out his hand. "We know you will do an excellent job, Samantha. Oh, by the way, Bobbie will continue in your department, of course. I'm sure she'll help you get acclimated."

Samantha stood and clasped his hand in what she hoped was a firm, professional handshake. "She's a very efficient woman. I'm glad she's staying on."

"And Jack, too. I assume you two are working well together, and there won't be any problems."

"No, of course not. He's a strong asset." Thinking of Jack's assets made her blush uncontrollably, and she feigned a cough to clear her head of the distraction.

"Let me know if you need anything."

Samantha moved to the door.

Joe stopped her. "How's the altruism project coming?"

"Very well. I have an appointment tomorrow with a manufacturer in Frisco."

"Good. We don't want the project to lag. It's very important to your father."

"Yes, I understand. I'll keep you updated as things progress."

He nodded and smiled. Samantha left the office and walked a few feet down the hall before leaning against a wall. She tried to steady her breathing. "Good grief! Oh, Joanna! I don't know if I'm up to this," she whispered to the ceiling.

And now I have to be Jack's boss.

****

"So, when are we supposed to be at Eco-Tek?" Jack asked the next morning over coffee in Samantha's cubicle.

"I thought I'd handle this one alone. It's not far. There's no reason for you to come, too." The last thing she wanted was to spend the afternoon in close proximity to Jack.

"Oh, come on. I'll behave."

"I don't trust you. Remember the coral incident?"

He laughed. "You know I was joking."

"Yes, I know, but I need to get my feet wet as the team leader. I need to do this one alone. Besides, there's tons to do here. Joanna's office is a mess and there are more files to go through. Get Bobbie to help you."

"Okay, boss, I get it." He feigned pouting. "I'll stay here and study all these files."

"Perfect, thanks. I'll see you later."

Chapter Three

Eco-Tek was situated on several hundred rolling acres of former ranchland north of Dallas. A massive herd of Longhorn cattle had once grazed there amidst pecan and live oak trees, drinking from the man-made stock pond now home to various exotic birds.

Samantha parked in front of what looked like a farmhouse, freshly painted and perfectly maintained. A small sign by the gravel drive said "Eco-Tek." A tall, blond man came out to greet her.

He stuck out his hand and said with a smile that showed straight, white teeth, "Steed Lambert." Dressed in a plaid shirt and tight-fitting jeans that slid over well-worn boots, he boasted the kind of rugged good looks that came from years spent outdoors.

His blue eyes shone warmly as he explained how his cottage industry made a limited line of clothes from natural fabrics, which now included a line of fashions created from recycled water bottles.

"I tried my hand at ranching after Dad died five years ago. I was lousy at it. But I'm a good businessman. So, I looked for an alternative way to use all this land." He made a sweeping gesture as if to include the whole earth.

"I'm so sorry about your dad," Samantha said. "But how did you ever get involved in water bottles?"

"While I tried to figure out how to utilize the land, I

became an environmentalist. I couldn't let my land and my home reflect one set of values and my business reflect another, so I merged them. Eco-Tek was the result."

His cornflower blue eyes reflected such sincerity that Samantha felt a sudden kinship with this tall Texan. She copied Steed's sweeping gesture. "Looking around here, I don't see much industry at all. Where's your manufacturing plant?"

"We started in the barn but outgrew it in a few years. I've had to set up a plant in a bigger building on another part of the ranch. I'll take you there after I've shown you around here. This is the part of the property where I have my office." He ushered her into the farmhouse.

"Goodness!" she exclaimed when she stepped inside. Slubby gray upholstery covered the sleek steel furniture. "This is certainly different from the outside of the house."

"It's part of the total environmental awareness that makes up our philosophy at Eco-Tek," Steed said proudly. "All the furniture in the room is made from recycled metals or reclaimed wood. The fabric surfaces are our own fabrics. Everything is designed for energy efficiency and comfort. Come on, I'll show you the rest."

She and Steed left the office and crossed the gravel drive to a traditional red barn, complete with hay bales stacked in front. Inside were the warehouse and shipping areas, where people scurried from huge bins and shelves to long tables, carrying packaged merchandise for shipment to retailers.

Steed said, "The barn has been renovated and insulated to maximize energy efficiency. The storage units are made from lumber fabricated from recycled plastic. It lasts virtually forever and keeps the plastic out of the landfills."

"What about the hay bales?" Samantha asked.

He chuckled. "I keep them here because I like how they look next to the barn, but we use them for the horse stalls."

"Horses?"

"Yeah, I have several. I'll show you."

He led her from the barn to a golf cart. and drove them up and over a small hill. Samantha gasped when they reached the top of the rise. Spread out below her, a scattering of buildings seemed to snuggle into the surrounding vista.

"It's pretty, isn't it?" Steed asked, chuckling. "Everyone's surprised by the view."

"It's gorgeous!" Tall pecan trees, oaks, and pines mingled in a lush column on either side of a gurgling brook running through a grassy meadow. The air was fresh and clean, and Samantha breathed it in, as if she were drowning. This was nothing like Dallas.

She and Steed spent the rest of the afternoon touring the grounds. He showed her the house he had built of cast-off tires, filled with sand and stacked to create thick, self-insulating walls.

Steed explained, "The house is covered in adobe. Between that and the tires, the only heating and cooling needed can be provided by solar panels on the roof."

Farther on he pointed out the plant, built much like the house but more extensive and open. Inside, people cut thick stacks of colorful fleece fabrics with automated machines and sewed jackets, pullovers, and pants by the dozens.

In a separate space, designers fitted garments on

lean models, pinning, and measuring. Samantha was mesmerized watching them work.

Steed led her into a small showroom where clothing was displayed on an array of mannequins. "This is a representative sampling of our entire line. We take pride in everything we make here. We believe our fashions offer value to the customer and also benefit the environment."

Samantha touched the hem of a woman's top. The fabric was soft and fleecy, lightweight, but cozy. "It's hard to imagine these were once water bottles."

"Then we've done our job right." He smiled at her, clearly pleased by her comment.

He was interrupted by his ringing phone and ducked into an adjacent room to take the call.

Samantha looked at the array of clothing options in the showroom—everything from children's tops to men's jackets and women's loungewear. She studied a child's bright pink jacket and was impressed by the workmanship and quality. She knew Eco-Tek's products would be perfect for R.L. Morgan.

She wasn't trying to listen, but from the other room, she could hear Steed's side of the call. His voice was heated. "That is not what we agreed to, and it's not in your best interest to change the deal now. I think you know what I'm capable of."

Surprised by his harsh tone, she wondered what the argument was about, but dismissed it quickly because he returned to the showroom, completely unruffled.

"Come on. I'll introduce you to the horses." He led her into another cavernous barn.

Steed said, "We dismantled a few dilapidated log cabins and reconstructed the pieces to form the barn. It's home to several horses, three dogs, and a couple of cats."

Samantha smiled up at her host. "This is positively charming."

He grinned back at her. "Do you ride?"

Samantha ran her hand down the velvety neck of a big chestnut horse. "Yes, whenever I can, but, unfortunately, it's not as often as I'd like."

"Well, we'll have to get you out here for a ride soon."

"I'd like that," she said.

"I'm completely amazed," Samantha exclaimed, her head reeling from all she had seen. They walked out of the barn into the bright afternoon sun.

Steed laughed. "My family thinks I'm a little out of control."

"Your wife doesn't approve of all these ecological wonders?"

"I don't have a wife." Steed paused, still smiling. "I haven't found anyone who feels the same way I do about the environment."

Samantha shook her head sincerely. "Anyone would be impressed by what you've done here."

Steed took off the Stetson he'd worn all afternoon and raked his hand through sandy-colored hair. "I have one more thing to show you—if you're interested."

"Sure," she answered eagerly.

He grabbed her hand, and they walked about twenty yards to the edge of another hill behind the barn. A slight wind came up to herald the setting sun. Steed continued to hold her hand when they reached the crest of the hill.

Samantha gasped. Before her, for what seemed like miles, were rows of sleek aluminum windmills, turning steadily in perfect unison. Against the pinkish sky, they were like eerie sentinels guarding the future.

"My God, it's beautiful," she whispered. "Is this yours, too?"

Steed answered her in equally reverent tones as if talking would make the windmills cease their rhythmic turning. "Yep. They generate tons of electricity. I store what we need and sell the rest to the city of Frisco."

He turned and looked at Samantha, his blue eyes warm and crinkling at the corners as he smiled. "So, this is what I did with the land. What do you think?"

She looked up into his tanned face, shadowed by the setting sun. "Your dad would be proud of you."

"I hope so."

When they returned to Samantha's car, she said, "We didn't talk much business, I'm afraid. But I really liked what I saw."

"We'll do business next time."

"Next time?"

"Yes, I'd love for you to come back."

"I'll look forward to it." Samantha drove down the driveway and out the big wooden gate, barely missing a black pickup truck pulling away from the curb. So lost in thought, she hardly noticed.

She'd never met a man like Steed Lambert—virile, handsome, a rugged individualist, successful businessman, and passionate lover of the earth. "Almost as if he'd been made for me." She smiled.

But what about the phone call? Was he also a ruthless businessman?

She turned into the parking lot of R.L. Morgan and ran inside to pick up her briefcase. It was almost seven-thirty, and the building was virtually deserted. She hadn't intended to stay so long at Eco-Tek.

Still thinking about the lanky Texan and their pleasant afternoon together, she came out of her office and ran headlong into Jack.

Again, there was that annoying heart-skipping thing. Samantha fumed as the heat of a blush crawled up her neck to the top of her head. Why was it when Jack was around, she was no longer in control of herself? Her body took off on these flights of fancy, leaving her head behind. Try as she might to ignore Jack Stone, something inside her refused. And so, she stood in the doorway to her office, heart pounding, face red as a beet.

At least I can speak.

"Hello, Jack." She was amazed at how clear and calm her voice sounded.

"Back from Eco-Tek?" Jack asked, a smile teasing the corners of his eyes. "Long meeting."

"Yes, as a matter of fact. There was a lot of ground to cover, literally."

"Hmm."

"Yes. It was fascinating. The company's owner, Steed Lambert, turned his land into an environmental paradise. He lives in a house made of recycled tires!"

Jack shook his head thoughtfully, "I'm not sure I'm ready for that. I kind of like the more old-fashioned ways—bricks and lumber for my house and good old polyester for my clothes."

She laughed out loud despite her frustration at Jack's lack of environmental awareness.

"Jack, you're hopeless." She gasped for breath. "Good old polyester? It's polyester that got us into this mess at the start."

It was his turn to laugh. "What? The world's problems are because of polyester?" When he regained his composure, he said, "Why don't I buy you a drink, and we can discuss polyester as the root of all evil." When she hesitated, he added, "We should celebrate your promotion, at least."

Her body began to say yes, her head screamed no, and her mouth proclaimed, right out loud, as if it had a will of its own, "Sure, I'd love it."

Jack drove them to Snuffy's, a dark and leathery place full of sports fanatics watching a big screen TV on the weekend, but it was relatively quiet after happy hour in the middle of the week.

The curvaceous waitress ambled over and asked what they would like to drink. She never took her eyes off Jack.

Much to her own aggravation, a little ripple of jealousy ran through Samantha. She had spent an intriguing and altogether pleasant afternoon in the company of a handsome cowboy who loved the environment and ran a successful business, but now she found herself experiencing petty jealousy over a man she believed was materialistic and superficial.

"I'm an idiot," she thought and deliberately turned her attention to the Bloody Mary the waitress set before her.

"So, tell me about the house of tires. How does that work exactly?" Jack asked, stirring his drink with a celery stalk.

Samantha searched his expression for the sarcasm she expected, but finding only benign curiosity, she answered, "They take cast-off tires heading to the landfill and stuff them full of sand, then stack them up as walls. They cover the whole interior and exterior with adobe or stucco and, voila, it's a perfectly insulated house. Steed runs solar panels for electricity."

"Wow, that's impressive."

Then she told him about the entire operation, right down to the windmills. Never once did he slip into his role as ecological smart aleck. In fact, to Samantha's complete surprise, he seemed interested.

"So, this Lambert guy sounds too good to be true. Any reason to think he might have any link to Joanna? Anything suspicious?"

Samantha wrinkled her nose. "One phone call."

Jack leaned in. "Yeah?"

"He got angry with someone on the other end and kind of threatened them if they backed out of a deal they had agreed to."

"That's not good."

"It was at odds with everything else he appeared to be."

"Interesting. Wonder who he was talking to."

"No way of knowing." Samantha finished her drink. "It was probably nothing."

Jack agreed. "How about dinner? Shall we order something to eat?"

For once, Samantha was in control of her feelings around Jack. "No, I can't. I've got a lot of reading to do for a meeting tomorrow."

"Too bad. It occurred to me we haven't checked Joanna's email or her calendar." He leaned over the table, a conspiratorial look in his eyes. "Let's skip dinner and head back to R.L Morgan."

****

An hour later, Samantha sighed and stretched like a weary cat. "There's nothing in her email or online calendar. Everything is perfectly ordinary." She logged off Joanna's computer. "We should probably get out of here. It's one thing to transfer files for legitimate business purposes during the work day, but another to be going through her office so late at night."

"Jordan told us to find out whatever we could."

Samantha argued, "I know, but the security guards aren't aware of that particular directive."

"Okay, okay. A few more minutes and we'll leave. We don't want to raise unnecessary red flags." He glanced around the nearly empty office. "Did she ever use a paper calendar? You know, like a planner?"

"There weren't any personal notes in her online calendar, so maybe. I hadn't been looking for one before. It's so old school."

Samantha rifled through the box of personal items she had been amassing and turned up nothing. She pulled out the backpack Joanna had in Key West.

"We've been through that a dozen times," Jack said.

Under a flap on the back was another pocket Samantha hadn't noticed before. She unzipped it and pulled out a folded sheet of paper.

She opened it and sighed. "It's only an agenda Bobbie must have typed the week before the trip to Key West. The usual meetings and luncheons and stuff, but here"—she handed the paper to Jack—"Something's written on the bottom."

He squinted at the scribbled note. "I can barely make it out. Joanna had terrible handwriting."

"Let's see. I had to read her notes all the time." She took the paper back and did a little squinting of her own. "It looks like 'Tuesday—9 a.m.' and the initials S.L."

Before Jack could respond, footsteps came toward them. It was probably the security they had hired to keep people from snooping. How would she explain her presence with Jack in Joanna's office so close to ten p.m.? No one ever worked that late.

Without a word, Jack grabbed Sam and pinned her against the wall, his body covering hers. Then he began kissing her with such passion she could barely breathe. The typed agenda still clutched in her hand was sandwiched safely between them.

Hank, the off-duty policeman hired for that rotation, stuck his head in and chuckled. "Working a little late, aren't you, Mr. Stone?"

Jack broke off the kiss to answer in a breathless, slightly frustrated voice, without turning around, "We're leaving. Goodnight, Hank."

The guard walked off down the hall, still chuckling.

Jack backed away from Samantha, still pressed against the wall, struggling to catch her breath and calm her racing heart.

Her embarrassment finally overcame the heat of Jack's kiss. "I'd rather Hank didn't think I engage in trysts at the office on a regular basis."

"You said yourself we're not supposed to be rifling through a fellow worker's office—a dead fellow worker's office— so late at night." He ran a hand through his hair, looking like he needed a little calming down, too. "Relax. There's no way he recognized you. You were completely…hmm…disguised."

Samantha had to laugh then. "Is that what you'd call it?" Jack's ridiculous ruse may have worked, but it didn't help her keep her distance from him. There had been very little distance between them during the kiss. "Bobbie will have a field day tomorrow."

Jack shrugged. "They'll chalk it up to my bad

reputation. While yours is still pristine." He bowed with a flourish.

She curtsied. "Thank you for your sacrifice, kind sir. You'll be the talk of the coffee bar in the morning."

"Everyone will wonder who my latest conquest might be. It'll do wonders for my reputation as a rogue."

"You know about that, huh?"

"Of course." Jack smiled, lifting an eyebrow. "I've had to work a long time to perfect it." He chuckled. "At least we have the agenda."

Samantha's resolve to stay away from him had flagged under the onslaught of his kiss, even though he staged it purely for the officer's benefit. Besides, her need to understand the scribbled note still clutched in her fist overpowered the warning bells in her head. And she was starving.

"How about dinner?" Samantha asked.

Jack hesitated. "Well, we could go to my place. I haven't gotten an apartment yet. I'm in one of those extended-stay hotels. But it's quiet and away from prying policemen."

"Great, let's go there. We can order dinner. I'll follow you."

"Better yet, I'll cook," Jack offered.

"Ooh, intriguing," she said, curious about his culinary skills. "And maybe we can figure out who S.L. is." She gathered her purse and the papers and then turned off the desk lamp.

Jack ushered her out the door. "I have a few ideas," he muttered.

****

Jack lived a few minutes from R.L. Morgan, in a 7-Day Inn outside the loop.

His place was a dump, clean enough, but not the kind of place he'd have chosen to live in if he'd had his way about it. Vince didn't think his operatives needed the lap of luxury, so here he was heating soup at night in the dreary kitchenette.

He noticed Samantha's grimace when she walked in. "I haven't had time to apartment shop. I've been a little busy," he said; then he lied. "All my stuff is in storage."

It would never do for Sam to know he was only here long enough to root out the source of the threats and neutralize them. Then he'd be heading back to Colorado. But she caught him off-guard, and he had to run with it.

"This is not what I had in mind for you." She crinkled her nose and ran her hand along the nineties-era easy chair.

"Gee, thanks! It's only temporary." Which was not a lie.

"I'm sorry, I didn't mean... I mean, I...oh, for heaven's sake," she stammered.

Jack laughed out loud at her discomfort. "It's okay. I know it's awful. Maybe you can help me find a place more...suitable."

"I'll settle for something from this century." She perched on the arm of the chair. "What's your style anyway, Jack Stone? Glass, chrome, Mid-Mod, Ultra-Mod?"

"You'll laugh."

Samantha crossed her heart with two fingers. "Promise."

"I like traditional. Overstuffed furniture and overstuffed bookcases, antiques, and a lot of houseplants. I'd even like a cat or two. Overstuffed, of course."

"Of course." She smiled and nodded. "Is that what your house in Colorado looked like?"

"I've never actually had that kind of home." He fingered the leaf of a fake ivy plant trailing across the fake mantel. "I've always traveled a lot. No plants. No cats. My apartment in Colorado is—was—pretty bare bones. Nothing remotely comfortable."

"That's too bad. But I would never have thought of you as the overstuffed type." She paused, then looked up at him deliberately fluttering her lashes in a teasing flirtation. "Maybe it's the rogue reputation."

He grimaced.

She continued, "What was your home like growing up? Antiques and bookcases?"

"Not exactly. My parents were killed when I was a toddler. I lived in one foster home after another until I was a teenager. Then I mostly got into trouble."

"Trouble? What kind of trouble?" Samantha moved to a stool at the kitchen counter while Jack pulled salad makings out of the refrigerator.

"Oh, you know, shoplifting, hubcaps, an occasional car bombing."

Samantha gasped.

Jack grinned. "I'm kidding. Nothing major, but I lived on the road, if you know what I mean. Then David found me."

"David?"

"David Thornton, a wonderful old curmudgeon who owned a convenience store I decided to rob one day."

"Jack, oh, no."

"It never happened. David read me like a book. He grabbed me and told me if I wanted something, he had chores I could do to earn it. I worked for him every day after that, finished school, and never got into any more trouble."

"All you needed was a job?"

"No, all I needed was a parent—someone to look out for me and care whether I lived or died. Someone to tell me no but give me an alternative. Then came David."

"You were lucky to stumble across him."

"Yeah, I'd probably be in prison by now otherwise." Jack shook his head.

"Where is David now?"

"He died years ago after I graduated from college. He helped put me through school and then got me into the Navy." He paused. "I've always wished I could repay him for what he did for me."

****

Samantha watched Jack slice mushrooms and add them to the growing pile of crisp greens and fresh vegetables. Her mind tumbled with this newfound information about Jack Stone. No wonder he was driven to succeed. No wonder he had little patience where weakness and whining were concerned. No wonder he was one of the strongest men she had ever met, as in control as her father, himself the product of a hardscrabble life. A warm sensation built in Samantha's chest, threatening to bring her to tears if she didn't do something fast.

She still held the agenda in her hand. She laid it flat on the counter and smoothed the wrinkles out. "So, what do you make of this?" she asked Jack as he poured two glasses of chilled wine.

"She was going somewhere on Tuesday at nine a.m.," he answered as he moved to the laminate table she had set with take-out plasticware and paper plates. "With someone named S.L.?"

Sam sat down and began filling her plate. "We ate breakfast together that morning. She didn't say a word about going anywhere. That's odd, isn't it? If she had arranged it ahead of time."

"There wouldn't be any reason to keep it a secret unless she were meeting someone…illicit."

"Like whom? Someone from the company? That wouldn't be unusual at all."

"What if it were someone from outside the company? Someone who wasn't even supposed to be there. What if she had arranged to meet her mysterious lover in Florida during the meeting?"

"The guy from New Hampshire?"

Jack nodded. "Then she may not want to let everyone know, but why? Did he have two heads?"

"Maybe he's a competitor? Or wait, Jack, what if he's a vendor—someone we do business with—a supplier, maybe? Then it would be important for her not to let anyone know they were seeing each other—major conflict of interest."

"That must be it. But why would she risk seeing him at a company meeting in Florida?"

"Maybe she was so totally in love she couldn't say no. Maybe he insisted."

"Pretty risky. Why would he insist? It would be as dangerous for him to be seen with her. He'd lose R.L. Morgan's business."

Samantha rested her chin on her hand, her eyes gleaming. "He had to see her in Florida because he had to kill her, Jack. Joanna was murdered on Tuesday."

"The note didn't say anything about where they

were meeting or what they were doing. Were they going snorkeling? SCUBA? Swim? She had on her bathing suit at breakfast… So many questions."

Samantha took the last bite of her salad and Jack grabbed her empty plate. He tossed it in the trash with his own. Then he joined Samantha on the threadbare sofa.

"There's something else we haven't talked about," Sam said, twisting her hands nervously in her lap.

"Oh, yeah, what's that?" Jack asked, draining his wineglass.

"Who is S.L.?"

Jack said, "So far, the only S.L. we know is your squeaky-clean Steed Lambert."

Samantha sighed. She had thought about it, too. "It can't be him."

"I think we'd better call Detective Jordan in the morning," Jack said, placing his hand over hers, stilling them instantly, and shooting tiny sparks of electricity through her fingers.

"Yes, I suppose so." Samantha stared at the strong bronze hand covering her smaller, olive-hued ones.

Jack searched her face, his eyes a smoldering gray. "Sam, I told you all about my checkered past. Now, I have a question for you. Will you answer it?"

She was hypnotized by those eyes. "If I can."

"Why are you trying to drive me crazy?"

Samantha had steeled herself for any number of questions, but not that one. She jerked her hands away. "What? I'm not trying to drive you crazy! Why would you think that?"

"You practically jump out of your skin when I touch you. You told me in every way possible you want nothing to do with me. Yet, here we are, enjoying a pleasant evening, albeit a weird conversation topic—I mean, it's not every day people talk about murder—but, still, I get the feeling you don't hate me."

She backed away a little on the couch. She needed space from Jack, his animal magnetism, his touch, his scent, and those eyes. She looked down into her lap.

Jack had a point. Her behavior had been all over the place. He had been nothing but aboveboard and honest with her from the start. He deserved an explanation.

At last, she spoke, "It's Gary."

"Gary? Who the hell is Gary?"

"My old boyfriend."

"What did he do to you?" Jack hissed, his voice tinged with anger and confusion, his eyes smoky and hooded.

"Calm down, Jack, pour us more wine, and I'll tell you about Gary.

Chapter Four

Jack watched as Samantha tucked her feet under her on the sofa and settled in to tell him about this ex-boyfriend who had poisoned her on men. He couldn't remember when a woman had so confounded him. It was as if this cat-like creature had bewitched him somehow. Since he met her, she had kept her distance from him, holding him at arm's length emotionally. But when he touched her...did she feel the electricity flashing between them as much as he did?

So why wouldn't she let him get close? Did it all have to do with this guy, Gary? He must have done a number on her to make her so skittish about relationships. Anger surged in Jack at anyone who would hurt Sam.

He ran his hand through his hair, mostly to quell his sudden burst of temper, and sat down beside Samantha. "Okay, tell me about Gary."

"It's pretty ordinary. No big drama or anything." Sam shifted as if she were struggling to get comfortable and gazed at Jack, her green eyes as brilliant as emeralds. His heart skidded, then settled back into a normal rhythm. That seemed to happen more and more often when she looked at him. *Annoying*.

"I met Gary two years ago. He was tall and handsome, intelligent, sweet, and successful in his business. He told me he lived in a high-rise on Turtle

Creek, but we always met at my place, which was fine, even though I like to go out occasionally. He said it was because he traveled for his work at an investment brokerage, and loved to eat a home-cooked meal. A couple of times when we did go out, he forgot his wallet. I don't mind paying, but I'd rather it be on my terms."

Jack noticed how she had begun clasping and unclasping her hands in her lap again. He wrapped his fingers around hers. She looked up, a vulnerability in her expression he had never seen before, and his heart wrenched with wanting her. He squeezed her hands and smiled, hoping to reassure her it was safe for her to go on.

She returned his smile and said, "He talked about how he had a big family who all lived in Houston and only got to see them at Christmas. I was surprised he didn't ask me to go with him that first year."

"Mmhmm," Jack murmured. He knew what was coming. He'd seen it before.

Sam continued, "The final blow came two days before Christmas last year. I had been planning for us to spend the holiday in Colonial Williamsburg. I thought it would be good for us to get out of Dallas and go somewhere meaningful and festive, just the two of us. Gary loved the idea initially, but as Christmas got closer, the more reluctant he became. Not openly, but in subtle ways like worrying about flying and concerns over leaving his business for too long." She rolled her eyes. "Then he started complaining of a lower back spasm. He wouldn't be able to travel at all.

"I got suspicious, started digging, and found out he didn't own a business. He's an insurance salesman. Also, he's an only child, still living in his mother's house in

Garland. And he was broke. He lost his money in bad investments. It had all been an elaborate web of lies designed to get access to my family's money and power."

She paused as if gathering strength to get to the end. "Over the years, there has been a stream of those kinds of men. Liars and users and ladder climbers. So, on New Year's Eve, I resolved to give up men." She smiled a little at the melodrama of it all, though tears welled up in her eyes and threatened to spill down her cheeks.

Jack didn't think it was funny at all. "What a jerk. What a spineless, little, weaselly jerk." Fortunately, the weaselly jerk wasn't in the room, or Jack would have gladly torn him limb from limb.

Samantha looked at him, her face expectant.

"Look, Sam," Jack said, taking her hands in his. "You know my whole miserable life story. If I were going to make something up, I would have done a better job. And you know where I live." He gestured around the modest motel room. "I'm not after your family's money."

Samantha laughed out loud. He loved to hear her laugh. It was like ringing bells punctuating the silence of the room.

"And I'm not Gary," he said, knowing full well he was lying to her, too.

"No, you're not him. You're the most honest man I know."

Jack flinched.

She shook her head. "I've been angry at Gary for a long time for using me and lying to me, but now all I feel is pity for him."

Jack lifted her chin so her eyes met his. "Sam,

you're an incredible woman, and you deserve a lot more than a relationship based on pity."

Her expression was so vulnerable, so trusting. And the urge to kiss her nearly overwhelmed him. It was what he wanted: to touch her, make love to her, to hear her moan his name. He wanted to care for her, protect her, and keep her safe, preferably wrapped in his arms.

But Vince's voice in his head interrupted the moment, echoing his threat, warning Jack of dire consequences if he got involved again with a client. Never mind that this was different. This wasn't momentary lust. This wasn't a mutual desire for pleasure...no strings attached. Yes, this was different.

"Samantha." He sighed.

"Yes, Jack," she answered, her voice barely a whisper, their faces inches apart.

"I should walk you to your car. It's getting late."

Samantha's eyes widened, and she looked at him in confusion. "What's wrong?"

"Nothing, it's late," he repeated. "And it's been a long day."

"Of course," she murmured, stumbling to her feet. "Thanks for dinner."

"It was nothing. I'm glad we got a chance to talk. To get to know each other better." It was a lame excuse, and Jack knew it. She had bared her soul to him, and he was practically shoving her out the door. But he didn't trust himself if she stayed.

"Sure." She grabbed her purse and jacket and left, letting the door bang shut behind her.

He watched her get in her car and rev the engine.

"You handled that well, old man," Jack muttered, shaking his head.

****

Tears stung Samantha's eyes as she struggled to see through the rain pelting the windshield. It was a relief to concentrate on the road and not on her agonizing embarrassment at what had transpired in Jack's hotel room.

He felt sorry for me after my pathetic story about Gary. What made me think I could share something so personal with him? He doesn't care about my love life. Why would he? He can have any woman he wants. He probably thinks I'm a spineless doormat. It's certainly what I think. No wonder he wanted me to leave. How can I ever face him again?

Tears rolled down her cheeks, unabated. At last, she snugged the car into a covered parking place at her apartment and dashed up the stairs, in time to hear the insistent ringing of her cell.

Her wet fingers fumbled the keys in the apartment door lock. Once inside, she tossed her belongings on the table and dug for the phone in her purse. A tiny spark inside her flamed, hoping it might be Jack.

"Hello."

The voice that answered dripped Texas honey. "Samantha, it's Steed. I thought you might want to go riding this weekend."

The little flame flickered out.

****

The driver of the black pickup truck parked across the street from the woman's apartment was sure she hadn't noticed him there. He'd been trailing her for days, watching from a distance, binoculars trained on her every move, following when she left her office or apartment. He didn't like lurking in the shadows, sitting for hours, but it was better than driving like a madman to keep up with her and her lead foot.

Not to mention he was starving. Surviving on power drinks and granola bars was not exactly his idea of a healthy diet, but there was no time to pack a dinner or even drive through a burger joint.

Hopefully this damned surveillance would be over soon, and he could enjoy a hot meal.

He watched her go into the apartment and saw the lights switch on. He could even see her through the sheer curtains, talking on the phone. He would stay until the apartment went dark, and he could be sure she wouldn't be going back out.

It might be a long night, but he was determined not to let her out of his sight.

****

The familiar ringtone of her phone awakened Samantha from a fitful night of dreams involving Jack, Joanna, and herself in SCUBA gear at the office. Groggy but relieved to be awake, Samantha dragged the phone to her ear. "Hello," she croaked.

"Miss Morgan," Detective Jordan said.

Hank didn't waste any time calling Florida.

The Detective continued, "Sorry to wake you so early on a Saturday, but I understand you visited Miss Levinson's office last night…in the company of Mr. Stone. Did you find anything of interest?"

"Good morning, Detective Jordan. We were going to call you this morning. Yes, we've been through the files and found nothing interesting. Then, it occurred to us she might have information in her online calendar or email that could help. So, last night, we went looking."

"Yes, of course," Jordan said, a trace of amusement

in his voice.

Oh, great! Hank must have recognized her after all and told Jordan she and Jack were locked in a passionate embrace. *So much for anonymity.*

"As a matter of fact," Samantha said, trying to sound as professional as possible. "We did find an agenda. It seems Joanna had arranged to meet someone the day she was murdered. The initials on the note were S.L."

"That's interesting. Do you have the agenda?"

"Yes."

"Could you email it to me this morning?"

"Certainly."

"So, do you know anyone connected to Miss Levenson or your business who has the initials S.L.?"

Samantha hesitated. She hated implicating Steed on such flimsy evidence as his initials. "Yes. There's a company in Frisco we're looking at called Eco-Tek. The owner's name is Steed Lambert. But we have no reason to assume he is involved in any way."

"We'll check up on him from here. Perhaps you should keep your distance, Miss Morgan."

"It so happens I'll be seeing Mr. Lambert later today. We're going riding. *Perhaps* I can do a little sleuthing then."

"I appreciate your help up to now, Miss Morgan. But you are to stay away from any further investigation. Let us do our job."

Samantha wasn't about to stop investigating, but he didn't need to know that. "Of course, Detective, whatever you say."

"Oh, Miss Morgan."

"Yes?"

"Is Jack Stone still working there?"

"Yes, why?" The memory of the preceding night caused Samantha to grimace.

"You should take him with you today." The phone clicked off.

Not likely.

The last person Samantha wanted to spend the day with was Jack. Shoving him to the furthest reaches of her mind, she spent the next hour drinking coffee and devising several ways to obtain more information from Steed Lambert.

****

"Oh, he's beautiful...and big!" Samantha exclaimed.

"Yeah, he's quite a bit of horseflesh," Steed agreed proudly. "But for all that size, he's gentle and one of the smartest horses I've ever had."

The massive animal side-stepped as the groom led him across the paddock to where the two were waiting. He was magnificent, Samantha thought as she ran a hand over his powerful neck and chest. The glossy chestnut coat was smooth and warm under her fingers. She reached up to stroke his proud head, then jumped when he tossed it suddenly, jangling the bridle.

"He's hungry," Steed said, handing Samantha a carrot. "I'm afraid I spoil them rotten."

Samantha broke the carrot in two and placed one piece in the palm of her hand. The velvety muzzle came down, snatched it up, and immediately returned for another piece.

"He's greedy." Samantha laughed, letting the horse have the second piece. "What's his name?"

"Turk. He's part Arabian, and it seemed to fit."

"Well, Turk," she said, patting the white star

emblazoned on the horse's sloping forehead. "How about a ride?"

Turk nodded and nudged her shoulder.

Steed shook his head in feigned disgust. "One carrot, and he's your slave." He ran a hand over Turk's smooth, muscled chest. "Where's your pride, you glutton?"

He helped her into the western-style saddle, then mounted his jet-black horse, who had been pawing the ground while Samantha and Turk got acquainted. She followed Steed through the paddock gate, across the road, and into the field behind the adobe-clad plant.

The day was brilliant. A dazzling sun warmed the air and the slightest breeze played in the pecan trees dotting the countryside. She marveled at the feel of the powerful animal beneath her. Though she was no expert, she had always loved riding and recognized Steed was right to be proud of Turk.

"I love this time of year," Samantha said when they stopped an hour later to let the horses rest under the shade of a massive oak tree. "We don't have very long falls here, but they are nice."

"They're my three favorite weeks in the year," Steed quipped.

"Even more reason to take advantage of it. This is glorious," Samantha said, spreading her arms as if to hug the whole world. Steed chuckled as he busied himself laying a plaid flannel blanket beneath a spreading pecan tree. He watched her every move, which made her even more aware of the unbridled maleness of him. After a moment, he stretched out on the blanket, the Stetson over his face.

So, she took the opportunity to stare at him,

appreciating his slender legs defined by the well-worn jeans that had memorized every muscle and sinew. She followed them down to stop at the equally well-worn cowhide boots. He didn't look like a murderer. But he did look like he could be deadly to her. She would have to keep her wits about her.

He sat up suddenly and his long fingers plucked a blade of grass, holding it taut then blowing across it, producing the faintest high-pitched hum, as if a herd of mosquitoes had burst into song.

"Where'd you learn to do that?" she asked, intrigued, and plopped down on the ground next to him.

"My dad. Here, I'll teach you." He plucked a blade of grass and showed her how to hold it up to her lips and blow across it, but when she tried, the grass only fluttered, soundless. On the third try, she was able to produce a thin squeak.

"Mmm, impressive." Steed chuckled again.

"Well, it's not exactly my instrument of choice." Samantha feigned a pout.

"Oh, what do you play?"

"I'll have you know I'm a virtuoso on the comb," she said, then laughed.

Steed laughed, too. "We'll have to put on a concert. We'll get someone to write music for us. Concerti for grass and comb. It'll be great."

She chatted with Steed for a few moments about nothing in particular, and then, when she had steered the conversation toward business, Samantha saw the opening she had hoped for.

"How far had you and Joanna gotten in your talks about us working together?"

"Pretty high level still. We had looked at a few

products that might be appropriate, but we hadn't talked numbers."

"So, you had met Joanna in person."

"Yes, a couple of times."

He shifted his position, and Samantha thought he seemed suddenly uncomfortable.

"Were you dating?" Surprised at the thought, Sam sat upright.

"Casually. It was nothing serious. She was a fascinating, intelligent woman. I was so sorry to hear about her death."

"Yes, it was terrible."

Steed picked up another blade of grass.

Samantha pressed on. No going back now. "Do you travel much?"

"For business, yes, quite a bit. You?"

"Same. We were in Florida for our yearly meeting. That's where Joanna died."

Steed shifted again. "I heard."

"Ever been to Florida?"

"As a matter of fact, I was there that same week. In Miami."

Samantha schooled her expression into a mask of mild surprise. "That's a coincidence, isn't it?" She smiled, hoping she looked innocent.

"Yeah, it is."

Silence hung in the air like a shroud while Samantha thought about how to proceed.

She took a breath and plunged forward. "So, that phone call you got the other day when I was here. I didn't mean to eavesdrop, but you seemed pretty upset." She paused, plucking tufts of grass from the ground. "I hope there's no problem with your business—equipment or something."

Steed jumped up. "Damn. That reminds me. I…uh…I have to go check on something." He jammed his hat back down over his head. "I…forgot. I have to go to the plant for a minute. There's a cutter giving them trouble. I said I'd look at it. Totally forgot. Shouldn't take long. Why don't you keep riding that way." He pointed over a rise to the right. "I'll meet you back at the barn in half an hour."

In an instant, he was astride the black horse and galloping off in the same direction he had pointed. Samantha stared after him, open-mouthed.

What the hell just happened? He certainly didn't want to talk about Joanna—or Florida—or the phone call. Guilty much?

After a moment, deep in thought, she mounted Turk and cantered over the rise Steed had pointed to.

She would call Jordan when she got home and tell him about Steed being in Miami at the time of Joanna's death. She couldn't believe he had anything to do with the whole mess, but it seemed likely he was the mysterious S.L. on the agenda.

She'd have to tell Jack, although she didn't particularly want to see him any time soon. But she didn't see how she could avoid it. She shook thoughts of him and Steed from her mind and concentrated on enjoying the rest of her ride.

At the top of the rise, she was surprised to find herself looking down into the valley where the windmills, planted like alien trees, were spinning quietly against the late September sky. She urged Turk nearer, fascinated by their surreal presence. Up close, Samantha could see they were made of sleek aluminum, each one as tall as a skyscraper. The massive blades whirled rhythmically, reaching to the heavens, then down to the earth.

A noise in the distance, like the loud popping of a cork, broke the stillness in the air. A tiny missile whizzed past Turk's neck. The huge animal started, whinnied, and reared onto his hind legs, pawing the air. Samantha struggled to keep her balance, leaning close to the horse's neck. Then he hit the ground at a full gallop, darting into the field of windmills.

Samantha tried to rein in the frightened animal. "Whoa, Turk, whoa, boy! It's okay, boy, whoa!" she screamed, but her cries disappeared in the wind.

She clung tenuously to the reins, struggling to keep her balance as the horse hurtled along. If Turk veered into one of the whirling windmill blades it would make short work of them both.

She screamed louder, but the horse had his head now and would stop for no one.

Turk's powerful strides ate up the ground, his thundering hooves deafening, He kept to the narrow path between the blades until he was through to the other side, never faltering until he was within sight of the barn. Only then did he whinny his approach, gather his legs beneath him, and fly over the paddock fence, landing gracefully with a shaken Samantha still in the saddle, much to her surprise.

When Turk came to a sudden and complete halt in front of the big, round water trough, Samantha tumbled over his head and into the water. She came up sputtering and flailing but unhurt. The big horse stood perfectly still, his sides heaving, covered in foamy white sweat.

Turk's alarm and Samantha's screams had brought

the groom running. Steed followed close on his heel. He lifted Samantha out of the water. She slid like jelly into his arms and began to shake uncontrollably.

"My God, what happened?" Steed demanded, scooping her up and carrying her into the barn. "You two look like you had the devil scared out of you."

"There was a noise," Samantha said, pulling herself together. "It spooked Turk, and he took off through the windmills."

Steed's intake of breath confirmed how dangerous the situation had been. He grabbed a saddle blanket from a railing nearby and wrapped Samantha in it, holding her close.

"I couldn't stop him. I thought he'd slow down when we got through the windmills, but he kept running to the barn. I suppose that meant safety to him." She shuddered. "Then he decided to jump the fence."

"I've never known Turk to be so easily scared. By a noise, you said. What kind of noise?"

"A loud popping sound. Like a firecracker."

"None of those are around here unless a kid got onto the property. They venture onto the land sometimes to cause mischief. I'll send someone out to check."

Samantha ran her hand across her eyes, brushing away her tears. She was calm now, and she knew no firecracker had spooked Turk.

"It was a gunshot, Steed," she said with complete certainty.

"Gunshot? Are you sure?" He looked confused.

"Yes, my father used to hunt. I've been around guns my whole life, and I'm familiar with the sound of gunshots. Especially a rifle. And I heard the whiz of the bullet go past. It barely missed Turk's head. I think that's what sent him flying."

Steed ran his fingers through his hair. "Well, I suppose it's possible the kid shooting off a firecracker was actually a poacher. We do have wildlife around here."

"I'm sure that's what it was," Samantha lied. She knew the shot was aimed at her and not a stray rabbit.

"I'll send someone out immediately. I can't have people running all over my property taking potshots at anything that moves." He pulled his cell from his pocket, punched in a number, and barked orders at the hapless soul on the other end. When he hung up, he turned to Samantha. "Let's get you up to the house. I have clothes there you can change into."

She smiled at him. "I think I'll go home if you don't mind."

"Can I fix you lunch first? I feel terrible about this. At least let me feed you." He looked like a little boy whose toy had broken on Christmas morning.

She handed him the blanket. "It's not your fault, Steed. I don't think I could eat anything right now. I need to go home."

He relented, but only when she promised to take a raincheck on lunch and let him call her later in the day. As she drove through the gate and down the dirt road to the highway, she took no notice of the black pickup behind her.

Chapter Five

Samantha's stomach pitched every time she thought about it. She was convinced it was a gunshot that had caused Turk's stampede, and she knew it could have killed them both. He could easily have run her into one of the enormous aluminum windmill blades, the barbed wire fence encircling the various pastures, or simply tripped in a rabbit hole, sending them both flying. She was grateful she and Turk had managed to escape unharmed. Even if she still harbored considerable humiliation at the way she had left the saddle.

But now she was unsure what to do about it. When she got home, she had tried calling Detective Jordan but found he was on a week-long vacation. There was no point calling the Dallas police since the ranch was in Frisco, and there was no point calling the Frisco police since they would probably think she was a hysterical woman who didn't know what she was talking about. That left Jack.

Why hadn't she told Jack by now? She knew the answer. Jack would go crazy. He'd accuse Steed of trying to kill her or, at the very least, of putting her in harm's way by letting her go off riding alone. He'd storm out to the ranch and traipse around to find clues. Steed would think she didn't trust him. And he and Jack would probably get into a fistfight. It was all too horrible to contemplate. It was easier not to tell Jack—not yet, anyway.

However, avoiding Jack at the office was challenging, considering she needed to work with him, and his office was right next to hers. She spent Monday ducking around corners when she saw him, rearranging her schedule to be busy elsewhere. Not only to keep from telling him about the shooting at Eco-Tek but because she still smarted from his rejection of her at his apartment on Friday.

That morning, she was trapped at the counter when he walked into the bustling office coffee bar. He smiled at her and gestured to her ceramic mug. "Trying to save the world one coffee cup at a time, I see."

Usually, the remark would have made her laugh, but instead, she saw it as his anti-environmental cynicism. "Better than your foam one. It will outlive you by five hundred years," she sniped, then cringed when several co-workers turned to stare.

Looking like she'd struck him, Jack threw the incriminating cup on the counter and walked away.

Later she found herself in a meeting with him and several others. Afterward, he lingered behind, pretending to pack his laptop. Samantha headed to the door. He intercepted her and said, "I'll walk you back to the office."

"Don't bother. I'm not ready for that kind of commitment, Jack." She swept past him and down the hall.

Immediately, a heated blush colored her cheeks. She was embarrassed and appalled at her behavior and at a loss as to why she seemed intent on being deliberately rude to someone she wanted desperately to like.

Tuesday, in her office, while she contemplated the

Green Earth file and tried to concentrate on its scant information, a dozen long-stemmed roses arrived from Steed. The note said, "When do I get my raincheck?"

Gazing at the flowers, Samantha let her thoughts drift to Steed—tall, sandy-haired, good-looking Steed, his honeyed drawl and laid-back attitude as attractive as the big cowboy himself, despite the suspicions he stirred in her.

But it wasn't Steed who caused her throat to tighten and her pulse to race. It wasn't blond hair but jet black, not a Texas drawl, but the bite of the northern streets, not crystal blue eyes, but dove gray that could harden to flint in an instant that made her heart lurch.

She tossed the file onto a stack of papers on her desk in exasperation. "For once, I wish I could like the nice guy!"

"What nice guy?"

Samantha looked up to see Jack framed in the doorway of her office, staring at her with his usual steel-eyed control. She immediately went on the defensive.

"How long have you been standing there?"

"Long enough to know there's some 'nice guy' out there. Let me guess—Mr. Roses?"

His sarcasm irritated her. "Yes, Mr. Roses—if you must know—is a very nice guy. They're beautiful, aren't they?" she asked, deliberately fingering their velvety softness.

"Yeah, great!" Jack barked and stalked down the hall.

Samantha jerked her hand from the rose, snapping a petal from the flower. It fluttered to the floor. "Why do I let him do that to me?" she muttered, picking up the discarded Green Earth file folder.

Samantha leafed through the folder, which contained a few references from their online presence and notes scrawled in Joanna's hand, but not much else. She paused when she came to a letter from the president, James Hoffman, inviting Joanna to visit the plant. The letter was dated February, six months ago. There was a trip itinerary for a meeting to be held in March. Samantha remembered Joanna going to see her parents in New Hampshire in the early spring. What she couldn't find were any notes dated after the trip.

"That's odd," she said aloud. "Why wouldn't there be notes about her findings on the trip?" Thinking she missed them, Samantha flipped through the file again but found nothing.

"Bobbie," she called to her admin. "Can you come here a minute?"

The older woman appeared in the doorway, notepad in hand. "Yes?"

"Do you have any notes from a meeting Joanna had in March with James Hoffman from Green Earth in New Hampshire?"

Bobbie thought for a moment, then said, "No, and I remember thinking it was odd there were none and no follow-up as if the meeting never took place."

Samantha thanked Bobbie, who ducked back into her own cubicle, leaving Samantha to think about whatever reason Joanna would have to keep her meeting notes a secret—or had she destroyed them? Maybe she had stashed them in another place, but why?

What was going on at Green Earth?

****

"I must be out of my mind," Jack fumed as he poured coffee into his new mug on Thursday. "Every time I see her, it's like having my face slapped, and yet, here I stand using a damned ceramic coffee mug." He went back to his office, shaking his head.

Samantha never left his thoughts for very long. It had been a mistake to stop the course of things in his apartment that night. He knew now she took it as a rejection instead of him trying to protect her battered feelings, not to mention a denial of his growing ones for her.

But when he tried to engage her in conversation to get back on an even keel, she cut him off with a shriveling remark. Her deliberate rudeness, which was either a defense mechanism or some kind of revenge for his dismissal of her, was harder on him than he wanted to admit.

And today was the last straw. When he stopped at her office and heard her talking about a nice guy, Jack knew it wasn't him. Then he saw the roses. Who the hell sent her roses? He could hold his own against a lot of things, but no guy could compete with roses. He'd have to find out who sent them—who this "nice guy" was.

****

Jack watched Sam walk to her car from his office window. Then he went to her cubicle and casually stepped inside. It was after six, and almost everyone had left for the day.

The roses were still on the desk, a lavish arrangement in an elaborate green vase, a big red bow and tiny white baby's breath peeking out from amidst a forest of ferns and greenery. The sheer size of it made Jack grimace, fighting a combination of contempt and jealousy.

He snatched the card from the envelope pinned to

one stem. "That damn Steed Lambert! I should have known. And what does he mean by 'raincheck'?"

He hurried to the parking garage and climbed into a big black pickup, revved the engine, and pulled out into the blinding western sunset.

****

"Turk hasn't quit shaking yet." Steed chuckled as he steered Samantha out of her office down the hallway a few days later.

"Well, neither have I!" Samantha laughed. "It was quite a ride."

"I've had my men go over the area with a fine-tooth comb, but they can't find anything. Certainly nothing to support the gunshot theory."

"What gunshot theory?" Samantha heard Jack ask as he came around the corner. Exasperated, she thought he seemed to be everywhere she went lately.

"Never mind, Jack." Samantha tried to ease past him, but it was too late.

"Hello." He offered his hand to Steed. "Jack Stone. I'm a co-worker of Sam's."

"Steed Lambert. I own Eco-Tek." He shook Jack's hand and smiled. "I'm trying to get her to buy our product line."

"Oh, that's right, the recycled water bottles." Jack looked at Samantha and smiled. "It's a remarkable way to conserve the earth's resources, and Sam says the quality of the clothes looks good."

"I could use you on my sales force."

Jack laughed his charming laugh, and Samantha's mouth dropped open. What was he up to? Then, in the next instant, she knew.

"What's all that about gunshot theory?" he asked

Steed with a coolness she rarely heard.

"Oh, didn't Samantha tell you? A noise that sounded like a gunshot spooked her horse when she was riding at my place last week. The horse took off like a bullet himself, nearly running her into the windmills." He squeezed Samantha around the shoulders. "Luckily, she wasn't hurt."

Jack shot daggers at Samantha, then gave Steed a look of shocked relief. "Yeah, luckily."

She rolled her eyes at him. *What a performance!*

"Anyway," Steed continued. "I got her to give me a raincheck on lunch. And I'm here to collect. Nice meeting you, Jack."

Steed brushed past him, his arm still protectively around Samantha's shoulders so she couldn't turn to look at Jack. But she could feel the daggers of his gaze in her back.

****

"What do you mean—you didn't want to upset me? For heaven's sake, Sam. Someone shot at you! I'm upset. I'm upset as hell!" Jack hissed.

Samantha slumped in the chair behind her desk. People crowded the hallways, leaving for the day, saying their goodbyes. Several glanced into her office, curious about Jack's raised voice. Bobbie stuck her head in the door and mouthed, "See you tomorrow." Samantha nodded and waved to her.

"Calm down, Jack. I was waiting to tell you until I talked to Detective Jordan."

"Okay, so, what did he say?"

"I haven't told him yet. He's been out of town. He only returned to his office today, and I haven't had a chance to call him."

"I would think telling Jordan you were almost killed would rank a little higher than having lunch with Mr. Roses."

"How did you know Steed sent the roses?"

"Never mind. We're calling Jordan now."

"Jack, be reasonable. Jordan's gone home for the day. They're an hour ahead of us."

Samantha knew she was buying time. It was five p.m. in Dallas. Chances were Jordan was still in his office, catching up on work after a week away. She couldn't put off telling him any more than she could keep Jack from finding out.

"Don't be silly, Sam," Jack said. "He's still at the office. The man's been on vacation for a week. He's got a lot of emails to read." He paused. "Shall I dial, or will you?" He picked up the office phone and held it out to her.

She grabbed it from his hand and punched in the numbers from the nearby business card, glaring at Jack as ferociously as possible. But he surprised her with his deep, chest-rumbling laughter. It was infectious, and she started laughing, too. In fact, she had to fight to regain her composure enough to tell the receptionist at the Key West police station to connect her with Detective Jordan.

Samantha tried not to sound defensive when Jordan questioned her about the incident at Steed's ranch. "Yes, I'm sure it was a gunshot. I know what a rifle sounds like. And the bullet whizzing past was no insect. Plus, there's the horse. He was pretty convinced."

"Horse? What horse?" Jordan asked, obviously confused.

"Never mind. Trust me. Someone took a shot at me."

"Well, I'll inform the Dallas police and have them investigate."

"I'm afraid the ranch isn't in Dallas. It's in a suburb called Frisco."

"Well, then I'll call the Frisco police," he huffed. "Oh, hell, I'll come myself. It's about time I went through what's left of Ms. Levinson's office. I've never been comfortable about the Dallas police securing the information. They could have overlooked something."

Samantha smiled at the gruff man's constant bad temper. She liked him in spite of herself. "I think you'll find Jack and I did a pretty thorough job securing her office."

She grinned at Jack, remembering his method of "securing" the office.

He grinned back.

She turned her attention to the phone. "When will you be here?"

"I'll catch a flight out first thing tomorrow."

"Let us know, and we'll pick you up at the airport."

"Fine," Jordan said. "I'll text you my flight plans." He clicked off before Samantha could say goodbye. She stood looking at Jack, the receiver still in her hand.

"He wasn't too happy, but I can't tell if it's because I didn't tell him sooner or he's mad I got shot at, and now he has to come here."

"Probably both. And I'm not too happy with you either, by the way." Jack looked at his watch. "How about dinner? I'm starving."

"I don't think so, Jack." Samantha hesitated. The last thing she wanted was a repeat of their Friday evening. Despite their obvious attraction to one another, their meetings always seemed to end in a fight.

Jack countered as if he were reading her mind, "Look, Sam, I know our last dinner was a disaster. It wasn't what I intended."

Samantha lowered her head so he wouldn't see the heated blush on her face. But he cupped her chin and lifted her eyes to meet his. She saw the usual glint of steel melt to the softest dove gray as he whispered, "I'm sorry if I hurt you, Sam. I handled the whole thing badly. I wish you'd give me a chance to make it up to you."

She couldn't refuse. No matter how hard she tried, it seemed Jack Stone could melt the metal bars around her heart. "All right, Jack," she said. "Let's start again…at dinner."

****

Jack drove them to the airport the next day. Samantha stared out the window, lamenting the loss of green farmland to concrete ribbons of highway and giant steel office buildings. She sighed.

"What's wrong?" Jack asked.

Abruptly brought out of her reverie, Samantha smiled. "Nothing. I miss all the grass and trees that used to be here."

"What price progress, huh?"

"Yes, I suppose."

He studied her for a few seconds, then turned his attention to the road. "You know, you belong in another time."

"You mean I'm old-fashioned?" She pretended to be offended.

Jack hurried to explain, "No, not exactly. You seem to have a connection to a time gone by. It's hard to put into words. It's a feeling I get from you."

"I know what you mean. Sometimes, I would like

nothing better than to put on a hoop skirt and sit on the veranda." She laughed. "But seriously, I feel a little out of sync with technology. Maybe that's why I'm so protective of the earth. It's like there's so little of it left." The rest of the drive was in companionable silence. Samantha marveled at how comfortable she felt around Jack.

When he isn't making me furious.

Her dinner with Jack the previous night had been pleasant and blessedly uneventful. Their conversation centered on work, world affairs, and the people in their lives, peppered with anecdotes that had her laughing often. She had deliberately stayed away from Joanna's murder, Jack's childhood, or her failed relationships.

Then Jack delivered her to her car at the office parking lot well before midnight and said goodnight.

All in all, Samantha concluded, it was a perfect, stress-free evening.

So, why did it leave her feeling less than satisfied?

****

Steed glared at Samantha, his rugged face a stony mask. "Why didn't you tell me someone might be trying to kill you? Didn't you think I'd take an actual threat to your life more seriously than a teenage poacher? Or didn't you trust me with that little bit of information?"

Jack had driven them to Eco-Tek straight from the airport. There had been no time to tell Steed they were coming, although Samantha tried texting him. It was no surprise he exploded when she introduced Jordan and explained the reason for their visit.

It hadn't occurred to Samantha Steed might be angry she hadn't confided in him. "Steed, I'm sorry. I didn't want to get you involved in all this. I didn't think there'd be any reason to bring the police out here. Detective Jordan insisted."

"So, if the detective here hadn't jumped on a plane and come all this way, I still wouldn't know there was a would-be assassin wandering around my ranch?" he growled.

Jack, his eyes flinty slits, took a step toward Steed. "Back off, Lambert, Sam is the one they're after, not anyone else here. She said she didn't want to make a big deal about it."

"A big deal about someone damn near killing her! You people amaze me!"

Jack was about to move another step closer, his fists clenched at his sides, when Jordan stepped between them.

"Okay. I'm the one who's making a big deal about this now. And I would like to see where this alleged shooting took place. If you two can calm down."

Steed took a deep breath and let it out slowly. "Let's take the cart." He took Samantha by the hand and led her to the waiting golf cart. She got in the front seat beside him. Jack and the detective squeezed onto the rear-facing back seat.

Steed slowed the cart to a stop behind the barn. He hadn't looked at her or spoken to her—stared straight ahead, his blue eyes hard as sapphires. Samantha reached her hand toward his, then pulled it back. This was not the time or place to try to make him understand. Not here in front of Jack and Detective Jordan. It would have to wait for later.

Jack clambered out of the cart first and looked into the valley of the monolithic windmills, turning silently. His gasp of surprise was audible.

"Pretty impressive, isn't it?" Steed came up beside him. "If I do say so myself."

Samantha smiled. "Especially up close and personal from the back of a galloping horse."

Jack spun around to face her. "You rode through *those*?"

She nodded, still amazed they survived.

Steed said what everyone was thinking. "If Turk had veered in either direction, you could have been killed."

"Who's Turk?" Detective Jordan asked.

"He's the horse," Steed answered.

"A quite beautiful, powerful, and fast horse, with a really mean streak, I might add." Samantha grinned at Steed, remembering her pall mall ride, leap over the fence, and final dunking in the water trough. Steed grinned back, his blue eyes warming.

"Tell me exactly what happened," Jordan said, flipping open his ever-present spiral notepad and quickly sketching the area.

"We were under the trees, close to the creek, beyond the forest to the far left," Steed began, pointing beyond the windmills. "I remembered I needed to go check a piece of machinery. I left Sam to enjoy her ride and rode back to the plant."

"Where's the plant?"

"Across from the barn. We drove past it. The big adobe building."

"That's the plant?" Jack asked, his eyes wide and questioning.

"Why did you have to go right then?" Jordan interjected.

"The caller said it was a piece of broken machinery and work had come to a standstill. When Samantha arrived, I got caught up in our visit and forgot. When I remembered, I figured I'd better take care of it." Steed paused. "But, you know, it's funny. When I got there, nothing was wrong. So, I went to the barn to wait for Sam. Then I heard her screaming when Turk jumped the fence."

"Jumped the fence?" Jack turned to Samantha, his eyes wide in disbelief. She shrugged.

"Mr. Lambert, who gave you the message about the broken machinery?"

"I don't know. It was a text I got shortly after Samantha arrived. From an unknown number."

"Do you still have the text?"

"No, sorry. I deleted it when it turned out to be nothing."

Jordan scribbled furiously for a moment, then said, "I'll have to check out your phone." He turned to Samantha. "Miss Morgan, what happened after Mr. Lambert left you?"

"Turk and I continued to ride in the direction Steed told us until we came to the edge of the windmills. Then I heard a gunshot, like a rifle, coming from the woods. A bullet whizzed past Turk's head. That's what spooked him. He reared up, then took off at a full gallop through the windmills."

The men were silent.

Samantha rushed to finish her story, "I couldn't get him to stop. He was too scared. We got through the windmills; he headed straight for the barn, then jumped the paddock fence, and came to a dead stop by the water trough. Then I tumbled over the top of his head."

She looked from one to the other, but no one spoke. Then, inexplicably, Jack began to laugh. Samantha tried to be indignant but knew Jack was picturing her in the water trough. Unable to help herself, she began to laugh, too.

Steed glared at Jack, then joined him, chuckling at first until he finally had to lean on the golf cart for support. The only one not laughing was Detective Jordan, who stared dumbly at the three of them.

"What the hell's gotten into you? She could have been killed!"

Jack gasped for breath. "I know, but the thought of the horse jumping over the fence and then tossing her into the trough… I'm sorry, Sam," he said, holding his side.

"I wish you had seen them," Steed said between howls. "Turk stood dead still, with Samantha dripping wet in the trough. Neither one of them moved. Like neither one believed what had happened."

She smiled at the men around her, a rush of warmth filling her. These men cared about her, and that was a wonderful feeling. Suddenly, she felt very protected and safe.

When Jordan finished asking questions, it was nearly noon. He declined Steed's offer of lunch and requested Jack take him to the R.L. Morgan headquarters to go through Joanna's office.

"Well, there's nothing here," Jordan grumbled an hour later as he slammed an empty file drawer shut in Joanna's office.

"No, the police sent everything to you except the few business files I kept. And the agenda we emailed you," Samantha said. "There was also a box of personal effects we sent to Joanna's brother, Steve." She paused as a new revelation dawned.

"May I see the files?" Jordan asked.

Samantha led the way to her office and settled him into a chair holding the stack of color-coded files for the altruism project.

Jack met her in the hall. "Did I hear you say Joanna's brother's name is Steve?"

Samantha nodded. "Yep. Are you thinking what I'm thinking?"

"Steve Levinson. S.L."

****

Jack watched as Detective Jordan stirred two packets of sugar substitute into his coffee. They were sitting in R.L. Morgan's office, Jordan's little notebook open on the table between them.

Morgan paced, his coffee growing cold on his desk as, Jack assumed, it often did.

Jack sipped coffee from his recycled mug and spoke first, mostly to break the tension in the room. "So, Detective, did Mr. Morgan tell you who I am and why I'm here?"

Jordan glared at Jack. "Yes, he did. You know, Stone, it would have been helpful to have that information a little sooner."

"I get that, and I'm sorry. But every time I could tell you, Samantha was there. And I had no more insight except what we told you, which was everything we knew."

R.L. spoke, "Except for the threats."

Jordan was so angry Jack thought he might actually see steam come out of his ears.

"Right," Jordan growled. "Except for those. I can't believe it didn't occur to you to mention those either!" He took a breath, probably to calm his nerves. "Do you have them here? I'd like to see them."

R.L. produced a manilla envelope from his desk drawer and handed it to Jordan.

The detective pulled out a sheaf of ordinary-looking papers and leafed through them. Typed in various fonts on regular printer paper, each one made a vague threat: Back Off Now, Stop if you know what's good for you, Don't Go Where You Don't Belong, Quit While You're Ahead.

Jordan held up one that said I Warned You. "And this is the most recent? When did it come?"

Jack answered, "A week ago. After Joanna was killed."

The detective resumed his leafing. "When did the first one arrive?"

R.L. answered, "Back in the late Spring, around the time we started working on developing the line made of recycled water bottles. They were delivered directly to Joanna by name. When the third one showed up, she informed me. That's when I called Bolton Security—in June." He paused and gestured to the most recent note. "This one came addressed to Samantha. My security team intercepted it."

Jordan stuffed the notes back into the envelope. "I'm taking these to the lab for testing. Should have done that when you first got them."

R.L. bristled. "We didn't think the police would take it seriously. No crime had been committed then." He gestured to Jack, frowning. "I thought the Valor Security people could handle it. Like that did any good."

A flash of shame heated Jack's face. His guilt at Joanna's death gnawed at him. She had been his responsibility. R.L. was right about that, at least. Now, all he could do was help find out who killed her and keep Sam safe.

Jordan said, "I'm not sure Stone could have prevented her death. There's no indication the threats were escalating so fast."

That's what I thought.

Jordan continued, "But I think it's evident the murder and the threats are connected to your business, Morgan. And I don't think they're through yet."

Jack jumped when R.L. slammed his fist onto the table with such force the papers scattered. "Look here, by God. You better get to the bottom of this and fast! My daughter's in danger! What are you doing about *that*?"

Jack said, "I'm literally next to her all day long to the point she thinks I'm stalking her. And at night, I follow her home and make sure she's safe. I've already put a guard on her apartment overnight. But it would help if we told her what's going on."

"No!" R.L. bellowed. "I already told you we can't tell her. She'd fight it tooth and nail." He paced around the room. "Do whatever you have to and hire whoever you need. But you, Stone, you keep her in your sights twenty-four-seven. I don't care how you do it."

Jack protested, but R.L. silenced him with a raised hand. "Look, it makes sense you can stay around her. You're working on the same projects."

"Well, to a point, sir, but she's traveling to see two of these manufacturers."

"Perfect, you go, too."

Jordan nodded. "I agree. Don't let her out of your sight."

Jack sighed. He was already spending as much time with her as she would allow. Getting her to travel together would be difficult, if not impossible.

Jack watched Morgan down his coffee in one gulp as if it were a stiff drink.

"Look," R.L. said. "I'll tell her I want you more involved in the projects, so you two have to work closer. Tell her I'm interested in you moving up in the company. She'll buy that. I'll even suggest you travel together."

Jack shook his head, still unsure about Morgan's plan. "I don't know, sir. She's a smart woman. She's going to catch on eventually."

Jordan stood, gathering his papers and notebook. "Eventually is good. We need time to catch a killer. It's not forever."

Morgan circled the desk and came within a foot of Jack's nose. "Here's the deal, Stone. I don't like this any more than you do. I'd like to send Samantha home with a twenty-four-hour armed guard. But you and I both know her. She won't stop working. And telling her not to do something means she'll do it to spite us both. So, you go everywhere she goes. Make up a plausible reason. Don't leave her for a minute. Understand?"

"Yes, sir, I understand." Jack reluctantly shook his hand. "I hope this works as well as you two think it will."

Jordan took a last swig of his coffee. "It has to, Stone. I think Miss Morgan's life may depend on it."

Chapter Six

Jack bounced in the back of the golf cart, surprised to find himself back at Eco-Tek so soon. Sam had told him over coffee the day before she was going out there to see more of their product line and plant operation. Jack told her he wanted to do some sleuthing there if she could keep Lambert occupied.

Not too occupied, though.

Although he actually wanted to snoop around, his going along was more to look after her than look over the products. A guilty blush had crawled up his neck when he'd made his excuse. He hated lying to Sam, even for her own good.

So, like a fifth wheel, he had followed the two of them around for an hour, feigning interest, asking questions, fingering merchandise, but all the while on the lookout for anyone or anything suspicious.

He could see nothing unusual at Eco-Tek. It was a well-run operation boasting innovative ideas and decent merchandise. Steed seemed like the real deal, passionate about his business model and products. There were no incriminating phone calls or abrupt withdrawals from the group to repair imaginary machinery malfunctions, and Jack felt like an idiot for suspecting him.

"Thanks for the in-depth tour, Steed," Sam said, her green eyes shining in undisguised admiration as he walked her and Jack to the waiting car. A little too much admiration, if Jack were honest.

"And I hope you didn't mind me tagging along," he said, shaking Steed's hand. The two eyed each other warily.

"Not at all. I'm happy we'll be doing business together."

Bringing their attention back to her, Sam said, "I'll get the ball rolling on those products we discussed."

"Any news on the gunshot investigation?" Steed asked.

Jack answered, "Detective Jordan is still working on it. But nothing, yet. I'll let you know if we hear anything."

Sam got into the driver's side of the car. Steed followed Jack to the passenger side, pulling him out of her hearing. "So, are you dogging Sam on your own, or is this an official assignment?"

"What makes you think I'm 'dogging' her?"

"There's no reason for you to be here, Stone. Total waste of your time." Steed's eyes narrowed. "Tell me, does Detective Jordan consider me a suspect?"

"I have no idea what Detective Jordan thinks. But someone did try to shoot Sam on your property."

"That doesn't make me the one who set it up. Anyone could come onto this land. It isn't heavily patrolled," Steed defended, struggling to keep his voice low.

Jack pulled away from him and moved to the car. "That's something for you to take up with Jordan. I'm just the bodyguard, as you said."

****

Samantha shook her head. "No, Jack, absolutely not. There's no reason for you to come to St. Louis."

Jack argued, "Look, Sam, I know you can handle Bottle Stoppers without me. But I think I can help you get more information about them. After all, St. Louis is an S.L. We need to find out if they had anything to do with Joanna's murder. I can't do that from here."

He was right. It would help to have him along on the trip. Two heads and sets of eyes were better than one, after all. Not to mention the fact her dad had encouraged her to give Jack more opportunities to learn the business.

I've never known him to take that kind of interest in anyone before. Jack must have made quite an impression on him in Florida.

"Well," she hesitated. "I guess we'll give it a go. Why don't you make an appointment with..." She flipped open the file. "Peter Delvecchio, their head of sales. As soon as possible. We've got to get this whole thing moving."

Jack raised his hand in a smock salute. "Yes, ma'am."

Samantha smiled as he disappeared around the corner of her cubicle. Part of her hesitation in taking Jack was having to spend several days in close proximity to him. She couldn't even keep her distance at the office. And now...

I'm doomed.

She shook her head and picked up another file on her desk labeled "Joanna." Flipping it open, she dialed a number written on the inside cover.

"May I speak to Steve Levinson?"

"There's no one here by that name," the man on the other end of the line said.

Confused, Samantha checked the number on the display. "Oh, I'm sorry. I'm looking for Joanna's brother, Steve. This is Samantha Morgan at R.L. Morgan in Dallas."

"Oh, hi, Samantha, this is Steve. Just not Steve Levinson."

"And you're Joanna's brother?"

"Yes, I am. But my last name's not Levinson. It's Boudreau. Joanna and I were half-sibs. Same mom. Different dads."

Not an S.L., a dead end.

"Well, that explains it, then." Samantha wasn't sure whether she was relieved or disappointed. But at least she'd devised a plausible explanation for her call. "I wanted to make sure you received the box of Joanna's belongings I sent last week."

"Yes, it arrived yesterday. Thank you so much for sending it."

"You're welcome. We're so sorry for your loss. We loved her very much here."

"Thank you."

"Could I ask you a question, Steve?"

"Sure."

"Do you know who Joanna was dating in New Hampshire? We want to send our condolences to him."

He hesitated. "No, sorry, I wasn't even aware she was seeing anyone. I've only been here recently to help my folks arrange her funeral. I live in New York."

"Well, if you think of asking your folks, and they know who it is, can you text me the contact info? We just want to send our regards to those who cared about her."

"That's very nice of you. We appreciate it."

Samantha said, "Goodbye," and hung up, feeling only slightly duplicitous about her reasons for calling.

Unfortunately, Steve's information knocked out one

of their S.L. leads.

It didn't look good for Steed.

****

Jack lifted Sam's suitcase into the trunk of the car he rented at Lambert Field, the St. Louis airport, then tossed his carry-on beside it. Guided by his phone's GPS, he drove to the Union Station hotel Bobbie had booked for them. They checked in, got their luggage situated, then met in the lobby to go to dinner.

Sam looked especially adorable in jeans and a cranberry red sweater that accentuated her auburn hair. Jack tamped down a sudden urge to run his hand through it.

Pamphlet in hand, Sam said, "This place is huge and there are several restaurants. Are you hungry?"

"I'm starving. A man shouldn't have to survive on a tiny bag of pretzels."

Studying the pamphlet, she suggested, "How about this one? It's known for its wings, and there are blues musicians playing every night." She and Jack walked the short distance and settled into a booth. After they ordered, the waiter brought two frosty beers, and they watched a guitarist get ready for his set.

Jack took a long draught, letting the icy liquid chill his throat. One beer, he told himself. He had to keep his head in the game to protect Sam. "Have you ever been here before?" he asked her.

"No, you?"

"Yeah, a few years ago. For business." He recalled that particular "business" involved a kidnapping, a hefty ransom, and a grateful heiress. Those days were gone. He shook his head.

"What's wrong?" Sam asked.

Unaware his expression had given him away, he smiled at her. "Nothing at all. St. Louis is a great place. If we can, we should try to go to The Hill."

She looked at him, her eyes dancing with curiosity. "What's The Hill?"

"It's the Little Italy of St. Louis. Like an Italian Village in the middle of the city. Pretty little houses next to quaint shops and delicious restaurants. It's very charming. I think you'll like it."

"It sounds perfect, and since we'll be here one more night, we should go there."

"Okay, it's a date," Jack said, then stammered. "I mean…not a date…date…just dinner."

Sam laughed out loud at his discomfort. "Certainly not a date-date."

Jack laughed, too, relieved they seemed to have gotten past the awkwardness following her revelations about Gary.

After dinner, he and Sam took a leisurely stroll to the Gateway Arch, enjoying a stop at the city sculpture park on the way.

"This is stunning, isn't it?" she asked, clearly mesmerized by the meticulously manicured park which was a vibrant blending of lush plantings and unique sculptures.

But Jack was oblivious to the statues or the gardens, watching Sam, the way she moved, the delighted expression on her face, the way she gestured. He could barely take his eyes off her. "Beautiful, yes," he said.

She must have noticed because she blushed and changed the subject. "So, tell me, Jack Stone, what do you want to be doing five years from now, ten even?"

Caught off guard, Jack answered from his heart,

revealing more than he intended. "I'd like to be married, in a home, with those two fat cats, and maybe a couple of kids. If I'm lucky."

"Well, I didn't expect that," Samantha said, gazing up at him, her emerald eyes soft and warm in the dusky evening.

He shrugged. "Probably won't ever happen. What about you, Miss Morgan? What's in your future?"

She shook her head. "The way things are going, I'll probably never get married or any of those things. I'll be an old maid, who does nothing but work." She laughed.

Jack argued, "Nah, some guy will come along and sweep you off your feet."

She looked at Jack and said, "I'm not getting my hopes up. I'll settle for the cats."

They walked to the arch, and Jack stared in awe at the enormity of it and the engineering that kept it standing year after year.

"Wow!" Samantha gasped beside him, clearly impressed also. "That's something, isn't it?"

"I'll say."

After a few moments, they turned and walked back to the hotel in silence.

At her hotel room door, Jack stood for a moment as Sam dug in her purse for her key card.

When the door opened, she hesitated, looking up at him. "Thank you for a lovely evening," she said. "I'm glad we got to explore part of the city."

"Me, too," he answered. Once again, fighting the urge to take her in his arms, he said, "Goodnight," and walked the ten feet to his door, feeling as if he'd abandoned her on the road.

****

Sam spent a few extra moments getting dressed the next morning before meeting Jack for breakfast. She didn't know why it was important to look especially nice but told herself it was to make a good impression on a new client.

Jack's appreciative gaze was her reward when she entered the hotel dining room. "You look like you could do a little serious negotiating, Miss Morgan."

Jack, dressed in his black suit, looked somewhat serious himself.

"I think we make a damn good power couple," she said.

Over breakfast, she discussed strategy with Jack and they decided she would keep Peter Delvecchio occupied while Jack did as much snooping as possible.

Jack received a text message that the car from Bottle Stoppers had arrived. They gathered their paperwork and left for the ride to the company headquarters.

Bottle Stoppers International officed in a glass and steel high-rise in downtown St. Louis. Not quite as impressive as the name sounded, the offices commanded a single floor and fewer than fifty people.

But they were very enthusiastic.

Peter, a man in his thirties wearing thick glasses, a plaid shirt, and a well-cultivated beard, nearly shook Jack's hand off and embraced Samantha in a ferocious bear hug.

He took them on a brief tour of the office, which included an encounter with the CEO, Thaddeus Winslow, "Call me Thad." Thad looked just like Peter, without the glasses.

In fact, everyone at Bottle Stoppers dressed like Peter—in flannel shirts, hiking boots, and cargo pants.

And all of them sported either beards or braids.

Jack leaned over to Sam and whispered, "I think we're overdressed."

She struggled to keep from snickering.

A couple of massive dogs named Fergus and Klaus roamed the offices at will. And there were no walls anywhere. It would be nearly impossible to keep secrets from anyone, especially from each other.

Sam and Jack spent the morning reviewing financial information and product samples with Peter. Surprisingly, the company looked solid, and the product fit the parameters Joanna had set out months ago. Their manufacturing plant was outside of town, so Peter arranged for them to tour it later in the afternoon.

She and Jack ate lunch in the staff cafeteria—vegan choices of veg sandwiches or grain bowls. Sam loved it, but Jack sneered in disgust. She reminded him about dinner on The Hill later. He grinned and pulled a piece of arugula out of his sandwich.

The lively lunchtime conversation focused on the company's mission to recycle enough plastic water bottles to help mitigate their effect on sea pollution, and everyone seemed one hundred percent committed to it.

After lunch, Peter, Sam, and Jack drove out to the manufacturing location, to meet the similarly attired plant manager, Tom Sawyer. "Not that one," he quipped when Sam raised an eyebrow.

Tom took them on a tour of the facility, which included the same operations they had seen at Eco-Tek: employees receiving fabrics and supplies, fitting and sewing garments, packing and shipping finished products. It looked completely normal and above board.

Samantha began asking the questions that were her

signal for Jack to make an excuse and go snooping. "Did either one of you ever talk to Joanna Levinson?"

Tom answered, "I didn't, but we heard what happened to her. In Florida, wasn't it?"

Sam said, "Yes, just terrible. While she was out snorkeling."

"That's so awful."

Sam pressed, "Yes. It's certainly tainted my thoughts about Florida. Have you ever been there?"

"No, I never have."

"What about you, Peter, ever been to Florida?"

Peter seemed surprised by the question. "Once, years ago on a family vacation."

"Oh, but not more recently?"

"No, why?"

Sam knew she'd pushed too far. "Oh, no reason, just idle curiosity, I guess. It was beautiful. I'd love to go back under better circumstances, of course."

"Of course."

"So, neither of you had any contact with Joanna before her death?"

"No, you're the first people we've spoken to from R.L. Morgan. We're happy you got in touch." Peter smiled, but the expression didn't reach his eyes.

****

Taking Sam's awkward line of questioning as his cue, Jack asked another employee, "Which way is the restroom?"

The young woman pointed down a hallway. "Past the break room before you get to the warehouse."

Jack hurried down the hallway, then turned into what looked like an office. He rifled through the inbox, then a few drawers, finding nothing interesting. He was about to open a file drawer when he heard someone in the hallway.

He ducked behind the door. When the two people came into the office, he slipped back out into the hallway before they turned around.

It was not strictly by the book, but Vince always encouraged Jack to take the initiative, as long as it didn't involve a woman.

He hurried back down the hall and joined the others just as Sam ran out of questions.

She thanked their hosts and she and Jack settled into the car for the ride back to the hotel, dropping Peter off on the way.

When she was sure the driver's window was up, Sam asked, "Did you find anything interesting?"

"Nothing at all. They seem squeaky clean. Of course, I didn't have much time, but I don't think they had anything to do with Joanna's murder."

Sam sighed and leaned back against the leather seat. "Me neither, except Peter seemed uncomfortable when I questioned him about Florida and Joanna."

Jack laughed. "Could be he just thought it was a weird line of questioning."

"I know. Anyway, it turned up nothing. They never spoke to Joanna, and they hadn't been to Florida. I don't think St. Louis is the S.L. we're looking for."

****

Samantha nearly squealed with delight. The Hill was all Jack described and more. "This *is* charming!"

Historic brick buildings lined the narrow streets, and a restaurant perched on every corner. Shops, delis, pizzerias, and grocers shared space with tiny homes. The red, white, and green of the Italian flag colored everything from street signs to fire hydrants. Outdoor dining areas crowded the narrow sidewalks. And a lovely little park provided a welcome green space. Diners and shoppers strolled the brightly lit streets.

Jack guided them to a restaurant he had researched online.

Checkered cloths and drippy candles adorned the tables. Waitstaff in long white aprons and checked neckerchiefs were helpful and attentive. And the food! Jack attacked his parmigiana, sighing his appreciation. Sam's enjoyment of her tortellini was just as strong, if less vocal. A violinist moved among the diners, and a wrinkled old woman handed Samantha a rose. Jack pressed a folded bill into her gnarled hand.

Lingering over tiramisu and another glass of wine made Samantha sleepy. She couldn't help but lean on Jack's shoulder in the elevator at the hotel. When they got to the room, he managed the key card and opened the door, while she leaned drowsily against the wall. She smiled her thanks and traced the rose down his cheek. "Night, Jack."

"Goodnight, Sam."

She disappeared inside and closed the door.

****

Sam came down to breakfast the following day, wearing sunglasses, feeling just the slightest bit hungover.

Jack chuckled when he saw her. "Big night, there, boss?"

"Shut up," she snapped. "How much wine did I drink, anyway? Ten or twelve bottles?"

He laughed out loud. "Close."

"Really?" The pain in her head made it seem

possible.

"No, of course not. You're just not used to it."

"Why don't you feel bad? You had wine, too."

"Only a couple of glasses. I was driving." He didn't dare tell her he didn't drink on the job because it slowed his reflexes and clouded his judgment. He couldn't risk not being able to protect her. Besides, he couldn't function if he suffered like she did now.

She picked at her breakfast while Jack ate with his usual gusto. Then she gathered her belongings from her room and met him in the lobby. He checked them out and sent the valet to fetch the rental car. The young man pulled under the portico and left the car running.

Jack was about to load their luggage into the trunk when Sam exclaimed, "Oh, my phone! I left it on the table in the dining room." She sank onto the nearest bench under the portico and whined, "Please, Jack, can you get it? I'll wait for you right here."

He rolled his eyes at the valet, ran to the dining room, found the phone, and headed back through the lobby to join Sam.

A blast rocked the building, and Jack watched in horror as the rental car burst into flames.

Chapter Seven

Jack flew to the portico, scanning the area for Sam. Heart racing, he found her ten feet from the toppled bench, struggling to get off the pavement by the driveway. Yelling for someone to call the fire department and an ambulance, he scooped her up and carried her into the hotel lobby, placing her gently on a nearby sofa.

Letting his instincts and training take over, he checked her out quickly, feeling for broken bones or serious injury. Finding none, he motioned for a nearby hotel housekeeper to come over. "Stay here. Don't leave her, and don't let her get up. An ambulance is coming."

The terrified woman nodded.

He leaned down to Sam and whispered, "Stay here. Don't move. I'll be right back." He kissed her forehead. "Everything's okay."

He raced back to the portico, searching for the valet. He was the only other one who might have been hurt. But about that time, another car pulled up, and the lucky young man got out, mouth agape. Jack hurried to him. "Keep everyone back. Don't touch anything. Help is on the way."

In the lobby, the desk clerk talked to a tall man in a suit. Assuming he was the hotel manager or at least a security officer, Jack went over and identified himself. "Look, this wasn't an accident. After the firefighters are gone, don't touch anything. The police will want to go over the area." He ran his hand through his hair and looked at Sam, still lying on the sofa. He growled, "It's a crime scene."

Over the next few minutes, the first responders arrived, sirens blaring. Firefighters put the fire out, and the police cordoned off the portico. Paramedics tended to Sam and decided she was unhurt except for a few bruises. Jack would have preferred taking her to the hospital, where it would have been easier to protect her. But the truth was, all he wanted was to get her on a plane to Dallas.

That might take a while.

****

After promising the police he'd show up at the station to give a report, Jack rebooked their rooms for another night. Then he took a wobbly Sam upstairs and made her lie down. He sat on the bed next to her, holding her hand, rubbing the back of it with his thumb.

"What the hell happened, Jack?" she asked.

"I don't know, but it's too much of a coincidence to think it was an accident."

Sam nodded. "But who knew we were here? And why are they after us? We don't know any more about Joanna than we did in Dallas."

"I know. It's crazy. We're not exactly a threat."

"And now they're trying to kill you, too."

Jack didn't necessarily agree. He thought Sam was still the target and he would be collateral damage, but he couldn't be sure anymore. The whole thing had gotten out of hand.

It was time to tell Sam the truth about who he was and why he was there. To hell with R.L.; Sam needed to know.

He stood and paced around the room. "Look, Sam, I need to tell you something, and you won't like it, but…" He stopped to look at her. She'd fallen asleep, copper hair splayed out against the pillow, smoky smudges on her beautiful face.

****

A few hours later, Sam awoke, her head aching. She sat up, only slightly surprised to find Jack napping in the easy chair across the room. Trying not to wake him, she went to the bathroom and rummaged for the pain relievers in her bag.

When she returned to the room, Jack watched her. "How are you feeling?" he asked.

"I've got the mother of all headaches, but I'm okay. It could have been so much worse." She shivered. "If I hadn't sent you back for my phone, we would have been in the car."

Jack rubbed his eyes. "Yeah, I think the explosion was meant to happen on the highway, a certain amount of time after the ignition was turned on."

"So, someone planted the bomb overnight in the parking garage."

"Yep." He stood up. "Hungry? I can order room service."

She laughed. "Jack Stone, you are a very predictable man. Someone tries to kill us, but you are not going to miss dinner."

He laughed, too. "I need to keep my strength up if I'm going to hang around you."

"I know, it's a dangerous game. Being with me."

He came nearer. "It's a risk I'm willing to take."

Their eyes locked. Her breathing slowed. He

brushed a strand of hair from her face. Then he took a step back and cleared his throat. "Why don't you take a shower? You're still covered in fire. I'll go next door and order dinner. Steak, potatoes, salad?"

"Sounds good." She didn't want him to go. She was safe when he was there. "Hey, why don't you open the door between these rooms?" His quizzical expression made her rush to explain. "It'll be easier when dinner comes."

"Sure." He grinned. "Come on over when you're ready." He unlocked the door from her side, then left to go to his room. She heard the lock on the adjoining door disengage, and then the door swung open.

"Hi," he said, sticking his head through the opening. "I'll close this while you dress."

"Okay, thanks," she answered and ducked into the bathroom.

****

While he waited for Sam to get cleaned up and after he'd ordered dinner, Jack made a couple of phone calls. The first was to Detective Jordan.

"What the hell, Stone? A car bomb?" Jordan was practically yelling. "How did you escape?"

When Jack told him about the phone, Jordan laughed. "Thank God for a hangover. It saved your lives for sure."

"I know. We were incredibly lucky."

Jordan switched gears. "Did you find out anything new? Anything suspicious about St. Louis? "

"You mean besides a car bomb?"

"Not funny. Besides that."

Sighing, Jack answered, "Nope. Squeaky clean. They claimed they hadn't been to Florida or ever even met Joanna. It was a dead end."

"Thankfully not."

Jack grimaced. "Cute. Now, who's the comedian?"

"I'm not laughing."

"You never do." Jack chuckled, picturing Jordan's signature scowl.

"Look, I'll call the St. Louis police and give them the low down. Don't worry about going to talk to them again. Take Samantha home."

Jack noticed it was the first time Jordan hadn't called her Miss Morgan.

What an old softie.

"Thanks, will do."

He hung up and immediately dialed Vince, who answered in *his* signature growl, "Stone, you better be making progress. Morgan's getting impatient."

"He's going to be more than impatient, I'm afraid. Miss Morgan and I were nearly blown up in a car bomb."

"What the hell? At the office?"

"No, St. Louis. We're here on business. It was our rental car. Someone rigged it in the parking garage."

"Damn. Anyone hurt?"

"No. We're fine. I'm taking Miss Morgan back to Dallas tomorrow."

"Should I send more operatives down there to back you up?"

"No, we're still trying to keep things under wraps."

"Someone obviously knows."

"That's for damn sure. I'm determined to find out who."

"I'm sure you will. You always do. But I don't like this, Jack, not one bit."

"Trust me, Vince. Neither do I."

He punched off his phone and laid back on the bed, throwing his arm across his eyes. "Who's Vince?" Sam asked from the doorway.

Jack jumped to his feet. "Uh, an old friend from the Navy." He was rattled, like she'd caught him with his hand in the cookie jar.

His gaze scanned her up and down. She had belted the hotel bathrobe over pajama pants and a T-shirt. Her hair was piled on her head in a way that belied gravity. "You look better. The soot was not your best feature."

"Thanks, I feel tons better. Did you order dinner?"

"I did. It should be here any—"

The knock on the door interrupted him. Jack ushered in the waiter, wheeling the cart containing their dinner, disguised under gleaming dish domes. A bottle of sparkling cider chilled in a silver bucket.

Samantha cooed, "This is beautiful. Thank you, Jack."

He quipped, "Presentation is important." He opened the cider and poured it into the accompanying wine stems. "I think we may have had enough wine last night. I hope you don't mind."

"I think that's very wise." She paused, suddenly more serious. "We probably need to stay sober and be especially vigilant. I don't know who to trust anymore."

"I agree. I wish I knew who tipped them off we were here."

"Only Bobbie knew."

Jack realized immediately who had spilled the beans. Apparently so did Sam, because they said simultaneously, "Bobbie!"

****

The next morning, Jack had coffee and sweet rolls

delivered to his room; Samantha joined him to call Bobbie the minute she'd be at the office. She set the phone on speaker and put it between them.

"Bobbie, did you tell anyone about me and Jack coming to St. Louis?" Samantha asked, trying to sound as casual as possible.

"Uh, no, I don't think so…except for a couple of people who stopped by the office. Hank, of course, and your dad, Miss Morgan. He came by looking for you."

"Anyone else?" Jack asked.

"Oh, hi, Mr. Stone. No, no one…wait…Steed Lambert called, and I may have told him. I hope it's okay. After the beautiful roses and everything…" her voice trailed off.

Jack scowled.

Samantha glared at him. "It's okay, Bobbie," she reassured the admin. "Anyone else?"

"The man from Green Earth."

Samantha looked at Jack, who asked, "Green Earth? Who was it? Mr. Hoffman?"

Bobbie answered, "No, he didn't leave his name. I said Miss Morgan would call when she returned from St. Louis." She paused. "Did I do something wrong? No one said I should keep your trip a secret."

"Absolutely not. It's no problem at all." Sam shrugged. "Thanks, Bobbie. We'll be back in the office tomorrow."

Jack added, "Oh, Bobbie. Don't tell anyone else where we are, okay?"

"Sure, Mr. Stone. I *understand*." Sam could practically hear the wink in her voice.

She hung up the phone and rolled her eyes. "Good grief! Now, we've gone off on a lover's tryst. Thanks a bunch, Jack."

It was his turn to shrug. "At least we have an idea of who knew we were here."

Samantha chuckled. "Yeah, everyone at the office, for starters, plus Steed and whoever made the call from Green Earth. It's a big field of suspects."

Jack checked his watch. "I'd love to go sleuthing, but we have a plane to catch. Meet you downstairs in half an hour.

Samantha refilled her coffee, grabbed a sweet roll, and disappeared through the connecting door.

****

Jack steeled himself for R.L.'s volcanic response to the news of the car bombing. He and Sam had arrived back in the office in Dallas, and Jack had gone to the big man's suite to debrief him before the company grapevine did the job for him.

"What in the holy hell is going on, Stone?" He paced around his office. "That's it. I'm calling the police!"

"Wait, sir, the police in St. Louis were called. They're investigating. And Detective Jordan has been informed as well. I thought getting Samantha back home as quickly as possible was best." He paused. "I can protect her better here. Plus, we have extra men guarding this building and her apartment."

"But she still doesn't know, right?"

"Not so far."

"Well, let's keep it that way."

"Yes, sir." A twinge of guilt stabbed Jack's conscience. He'd almost told Sam the truth in St. Louis, and he still thought it was the right thing to do. He wished the moment hadn't slipped away. If only she hadn't fallen asleep. If only the car hadn't blown up. If only…Keeping his identity and his true job away from her was proving more difficult than Jack had worried about before St. Louis. Every time he was alone with Sam, he wanted to tell her the truth, to throw himself on her mercy, and then kiss her senseless.

She would be furious and hurt to find out he had lied. He could handle her anger. But the hurt…he couldn't stand to hurt her. She may never forgive him even now for betraying her trust, but every day he perpetuated the lie made things even worse.

He would have to tell her and soon. R.L. be damned. But when?

****

Samantha pinned the last three-by-five card to her cubicle wall and stepped back to admire her handiwork.

"What's all this?" Jack said from behind her.

"Where have you been?" His disappearance all morning had given her a chance to build her "evidence board," as she was calling it.

He hesitated. "Your dad called me into his office to talk, and I thought I should tell him about the car before he hears about it on the 'Bobbie Grapevine.' "

"Oh, no, Jack!" She started to tell him what a bad idea that was, then realized he was right. "Did he explode worse than the car?"

"Pretty much, but I doused him in water, so it's all good."

Samantha stared at him, then burst out laughing. The picture of her smoldering father was too perfect. "What did he want to talk to you about?"

Jack seemed hesitant, embarrassed even. "Uh, I think it was the same thing he told you before we left. He wants me to take on more responsibility and learn more about the business."

Samantha found his humility refreshing. In her experience, most men were arrogant, ambitious, and impatient to move up the corporate ladder. Jack didn't seem at all aggressive about the business.

Shifting her thoughts back to their investigation, she said, "What do you think about my board?"

Jack sat in the office chair, propping his feet on the desk. "Very impressive. You've covered all our suspects and suspicions, plus the…incidents."

She giggled. "I know it's a lot, but geez, Jack, look at what's happened."

"Yeah, it's a lot, all right, and except for Joanna, everything seems to be aimed at you."

"I know, but I have a plan. I want to go to New Hampshire…alone."

Jack leaped to his feet. "God, no! Absolutely not! I don't want you to go anywhere alone. Not even in Dallas. I can't let you go to New Hampshire alone! Are you crazy?"

"Calm down, for heaven's sake!" Samantha expected him to argue, but his reaction smacked of panic. Where was that coming from? "Look, Jack, let's talk about it for a second. If I *am* the target, then I need to put myself out there. If I go up there without you to run interference, they'll tip their hand."

Jack sputtered his displeasure, shaking his head. "No, this is insane. You're a target, all right, and you're going to get yourself killed."

"I'm trying to lure them out in the open. We don't even know who it is. Green Earth may have no part in this at all."

"They seem to find you no matter where you are.

You can't take that kind of chance. Let me go with you, at least."

"Too late." She shrugged. "Bobbie's booked me on a flight out tomorrow. I called Hoffman. They're expecting me the day after."

Jack stepped closer to her, his breath hot on her face. "No, Sam, you can't go without me. It's a terrible idea. I won't let you do it."

She glared up at him, letting her expression freeze over. "It's none of your business what I do, Jack. I'm a grown-ass woman, and if I want to go to New Hampshire alone, then I will damn well do it."

When he didn't say anything, she took a step back. "You can hold down the fort here. There's a lot of follow-up to do regarding Eco-Tek and Bottle Stoppers. You can take care of that while I'm gone."

"You've got to be kidding," he growled.

"I'm sure that's what my dad would want you to be doing." Signaling the end of the conversation, she sat down at her desk and began typing nonsense into her computer. She knew Jack wasn't happy about her plan.

He stomped out of her office and into his next door. The wall between them rattled when he slammed his fist into it.

Not happy at all.

****

Bobbie's eyes widened to round saucers. "You want me to what? Mr. Stone, I can't do that!" The tiny woman shook her head so hard the bun on top of it threatened to fall off.

"You have to, Bobbie; I have to get on the plane to New Hampshire with Sam. But she can't know." Jack needed Bobbie's cooperation to book a seat on the same flight Sam was on. And he had to work fast because he knew she was leaving town later in the day.

"Mr. Stone, why don't you tell Miss Morgan you're going along? Then I won't have to keep it a secret. I'm a terrible secret-keeper." The secretary looked so anguished Jack hesitated for a moment, then remembered he was weaving this tangled web to protect Sam.

"I can't tell her, Bobbie. It would ruin everything."

"Ruin what?" Her eyes lit up. "Have you got a surprise for Miss Morgan?"

Jack swallowed, then lied, "Yes, an important surprise. The kind of surprise you wouldn't want to spoil."

"Oh, Mr. Stone! Is it what I'm thinking? If that's what it is, I won't tell a soul! I swear. This is so exciting. Miss Morgan's getting engaged!" She clapped her hands together, and tears welled up in her eyes.

Jack shoved the wad of guilt in his chest a little deeper. Might as well press his advantage since Bobbie had given him the perfect excuse. He winked at her. "So, now you see why I want to go to New Hampshire. It would be a very romantic surprise, don't you think?"

"Yes, I do. Okay, here's her itinerary. It has the flight listed here, see? I'll book you a seat somewhere away from her so you can sneak on. How's that?"

"You're an angel." Jack grinned.

Bobbie beamed.

As he left the office, Jack knew this wasn't exactly what R.L. Morgan had in mind when he ordered Jack to guard Samantha. And if Vince ever got wind of this cockamamie ruse, Jack's career would be over. But it was all inevitable. The rumor mill at the company was a well-oiled machine. Before tomorrow night, the story would be out in every distorted form imaginable, thanks to Bobbie's self-confessed inability to keep a secret. Not that it would matter anyway, he thought with gallows humor as he went home to pack. Samantha would strangle him when he got to New Hampshire long before her father or Vince could get hold of him.

Chapter Eight

The plane lurched as Jack reached for the drink the flight attendant offered. He loved flying. The feeling of controlling a giant machine, harnessing its power, and matching its strength with knowledge, experience, and intuition. But that was when he was the pilot.

Not when he sat here like a sardine in a can full of a couple hundred others, having absolutely no control.

Lately, he knew he had lost control over everything. He struggled to do his job. He struggled to find the source of the threats and failed to protect Sam…twice. Now she was on this plane hurtling toward certain danger, crazy-stubborn about her stupid "plan" and running off without him to keep her safe.

He finished the drink and leaned his head against the back of the seat, letting his muscles ease. Avoiding her at the airport had been easy enough, but he hadn't realized how tense it had made him.

He had seen her immediately at the ticket counter, dressed impeccably in navy pants and a white blouse, a camel coat slung over her arm. Her hair gleamed in the sunlight streaming through the plate glass windows, reminding him of chestnuts, autumn leaves, and honey all mixed together. He had a sudden urge to reach out and touch her but ducked instead behind a nearby pillar, pretending to look at his phone. When he saw her head toward security, he followed her at a safe distance.

After he got through security, he headed to the gate, scanning the stores and restaurants for her. When he spied her in the snack shop, he hid behind another pillar until she came out, the latest best-selling paperback in her hand.

As it turned out, Bobbie had been forced to book him into first class since the plane was full. It was a stroke of luck since Jack could wait until after Samantha, riding in business class, disappeared through the doorway before he boarded himself.

Settling back against the roomy seat, he stretched his legs into the aisle, grateful for the additional room. He was relieved to have that cloak-and-dagger nonsense behind him. No matter what happened now, at least he would meet Samantha when the plane landed, and she would have to get used to it.

Sure. She's going to be furious, and you know it.

It might be well worth incurring her wrath to spend more time with her alone. It seemed to Jack their entire relationship had been a roller-coaster of emotion and turmoil. Yes, he thought, remembering the chaos after the car bomb, he and Sam could use the peace and quiet of the beautiful forests of New Hampshire.

As long as no one tries to kill her.

He had been to New England in October once before. A drop-dead gorgeous heiress he was protecting had invited him to her country estate. They were there to witness the spectacular season known simply as "Foliage" when the trees were festooned in leaves of burnt orange and amber, mustard, pumpkin, cinnamon, and every other spice imaginable.

Buses packed with elderly tourists invaded every village and hamlet, ready to pay homage to the resplendent work of nature and significantly increase the coffers of the long-suffering locals.

Jack had enjoyed the weekend in the woods, if not the heiress. She was merely one in a long line of beautiful women who had failed to move him. He smiled at the memory of her lovely face when he told her he'd be heading back to Colorado…alone.

"You can't be serious, Jack," she had argued. "You can't survive in Colorado. You'll be back in New York inside a month. And I'll be waiting."

He wondered idly as he drifted off to sleep if she was still waiting. It had been two years. He hoped not.

An hour and a half later, the flight attendant leaned over him. "Mr. Stone, we'll be landing in Boston in a few minutes. Please raise your seat and tray table to their full, upright positions."

Still groggy, Jack did as he was told, orienting himself by looking out the window to his left. Below, Boston unfolded on their approach. Then he saw the airport beneath them, incongruously perched on a peninsula jutting into the harbor. The grinding of the landing gear and the high-pitched whine of the flaps were familiar to him. The bumping and shuddering as throttles were ratcheted back and brakes applied were like songs he knew by heart. In a moment, the plane would slow gracefully and proceed to the appointed gate. And he would confront Sam.

Jack gathered his belongings from under his feet. Sam wasn't going to take kindly to his being there. If he got off the plane before her, he could meet her in the relative safety of the gate lounge rather than the first-class aisle and avoid making too much of a scene.

As soon as the seat belt sign went off, he retrieved

his carry-on bag from the overhead, moved to the cabin door, smiled hurriedly at the attendant as she handed him his trench coat, and then practically ran down the ramp to the lounge.

He glanced over his shoulder to check for Sam and neglected to see the woman in front of him had stopped. He slammed into her huge backpack and umbrella. The ensuing carnage found Jack sprawled on top of her on the ground, and bags and backpacks everywhere. However, she maintained her grip on the umbrella, which she brought down on Jack's head.

He struggled to his feet as several bystanders helped the woman to stand.

"Jack!"

He spun toward the voice—Sam's, of course—in time to catch a glancing blow from Umbrella Woman across his face. Knocked off balance, he dropped to his knees, blood oozing from a small cut on his cheek.

A nearby security officer hurried over and took Umbrella Woman and her offending weapon to an opposite corner of the gate lounge before she could rain any more blows on Jack's head.

He looked up to see Sam pulling a tissue from her purse. She dabbed it on the cut.

"It's already swelling. We'll need a little ice. Come on." She took him by the hand and helped him get to his feet. She found his carry-on bag and coat and led him into the nearest bar.

He sat at a tiny table and gingerly touched his cheek with one finger. It hurt. So much for avoiding a scene, he grimaced inwardly, thinking how ridiculous he must have looked sprawled on top of the hapless woman. And so far Sam hadn't said anything at all, as if it were perfectly normal for him to show up in an airport nearly two thousand miles from home.

She returned in a moment carrying a cup of ice and two tall, cool drinks.

"Here, sip this." She handed him a drink, and their fingers brushed, a palpable electric charge passing between them. Samantha jerked her hand back.

She wrapped a piece of ice in a paper napkin and gently held it to his cheek. But the expression on her face was as hard as her touch was soft. Glaring at him with fiery emerald eyes, she spoke in measured tones, "Now, why don't you tell me exactly what the hell you're doing here?"

Jack took the ice away from his face, drained his drink, and looked squarely into Sam's beautiful eyes. Unexpressed anger still smoldered in them. So, he mused, she wasn't as calm as she appeared. Better not to upset her further with the news he was her reluctant bodyguard. Judging by the look on her face, that would be the last thing she'd want. He took her hand in his and stepped headlong into the lie.

"It's your dad's fault. He found out you were coming without me and pitched a fit. Said I needed to learn more about the business, the product, and the manufacturers. You were already heading to the airport, so I had to haul ass to get there. I barely made the plane."

Her expression softened. "Well, I guess it's okay if Dad told you to, but how did he…never mind. Bobbie's Grapevine."

"I'm sorry. I didn't want to go against your orders. I know you wanted to come alone."

She sighed. "He's never going to let me grow up. I'm afraid part of him pushing you is feeling like I need protection from…from…life."

"I think maybe he's a little worried, given people are trying to kill you."

She shrugged. "I suppose." She studied her drink, then looked up at Jack, her eyes glistening. "Who was that horrible umbrella woman, anyway? And why was she intent on killing *you*?"

"No one. I stumbled into her trying to get off the plane before you saw me."

"I'm afraid I couldn't miss you—" She laughed a little. "—You made quite a picture."

"So, you're not furious at me for coming?"

Samantha turned away from him to look out the darkened window of the bar. A man in an orange jumpsuit, signaling with electric lights, guided a jet to the gate.

When she turned back, a single tear rolled down her face. She reached up a tentative hand and wiped it away. "No, Jack, I'm glad you're here," she said.

The guilt inside him turned to something else. Something he couldn't name, and he wished he'd never come to New Hampshire.

****

Samantha stretched her legs and leaned back against the comfortable seat of the luxury car Jack rented for their drive to Meredith.

"Two hours both ways. We might as well enjoy it," Jack said when they walked to the car rental desk at the airport. Samantha didn't argue. She was still too stunned Jack was there to think about company budgets.

Anyway, she was glad he had insisted on a big car. Even fully extended, her long legs had ample room—a welcome change from the cramped accommodations on the plane, which raised the question, "Where were you on the plane, Jack? I didn't see you."

"I had to sit in First Class. It was the only seat left."

"Oh, too bad. You were in First Class enjoying champagne while I suffered the inequities of Business. I'm going to kill Bobbie," she joked.

Jack looked uncomfortable and adjusted the air vent. "Is it hot in here, or is it me?"

Samantha laughed. "Oh, relax, Jack, I'm teasing you. And you certainly deserve it after you followed me up here uninvited."

"I suppose that's true."

Samantha settled in for the ride, enjoying the view, commenting now and then on the scenery. The drive carried them through the heart of Boston, then out into the countryside, north through Massachusetts, and into New Hampshire. In this part of the country, the interstate was a twisting ribbon, weaving its way through thick forests of birch, maples, and fir. Only the occasional green exit signs on the Interstate indicated civilization lurked behind the trees.

And the trees! Samantha thought she had never seen anything more incredibly beautiful than the impressionistic vision unfolding along the road. She was reminded of crayon colors from her youth: burnt umber, saffron, paprika, magenta, and goldenrod. All splashed liberally in a riot of hues unrivaled by anything mere mortals could have produced on canvas or paper.

Tiny exclamations of delight gave way to shrieks of pleasure as they came upon one spectacular scene after another. Even Jack enjoyed the gift Mother Nature had bestowed upon them, whistling his appreciation.

It was mid-afternoon when they turned off the

interstate onto a narrower two-lane highway snaking its way through ever-thickening trees. The sun was beginning its descent when Samantha caught her first glimpse of Lake Winnipesaukee, surrounded by forests, glittering like a diamond nestled in a sea of vibrant gemstones. It was massive even by Texas standards, and she thought it looked more like an ocean than a lake.

At last, they burst through the forest at the lake's edge. To the left, the tiny town of Meredith tumbled down a hill and stopped in a jumble of docks and boats at the water's edge. To the right, a colorful array of clapboard houses dotted the lake's rim.

"Oh, it's charming!" Samantha gushed.

The little village was picture-perfect. American flags, pots of fall flowers, and signs proclaiming "Welcome Friends" bedecked the colorful homes, shops, churches, and offices. Cars jammed the narrow streets, and tourists overflowed the sidewalks. How could so many people fit in one tiny town?

Jack eased the car up Main Street and into the circular drive marking the entrance to the Country Mill and Inn, where Bobbie had made a reservation for Samantha.

The inn was a deserted, turn-of-the-century cotton mill, boasting reclaimed and restored white clapboard siding, dusty red, shingled roofs, and multi-paned and clerestory windows. The whole complex was snuggled into the lush New Hampshire forests alongside the village of Meredith, overlooking a tiny finger of Lake Winnipesaukee.

Sandwiched between two tour buses, Samantha watched from the car as a sea of white-haired travelers disembarked from a day of shopping, judging by the numerous parcels they carried. She and Jack followed them into the inn.

"Welcome to the Country Mill and Inn," the friendly desk clerk said.

"Thank you," Samantha replied. "I have a reservation. Samantha Morgan."

The young man typed in the name on his computer. "Yes, Miss Morgan. You're in two-o-five, upstairs and to the right." He glanced at Jack. "But I'm afraid we have you down as a single."

Samantha blushed slightly, then hurried to explain. "No, no, Mr. Stone is in his own room."

The clerk turned to Jack. "What was your name, sir?"

"Jack Stone, but I don't think you have a reservation. I wasn't sure which hotel we were coming to, so I didn't book a room."

Samantha stared at him. "You got Bobbie to get you on the plane, but you didn't get her to get you a room?"

"It's not a problem. I planned to get one when we got here. We're here. And now I would like a room," he said.

"I'm sorry, sir, but we're booked. It's Foliage," he said simply as if that was all the explanation needed. Foliage was definitely a tourist draw, judging by the number of buses in the parking lot.

Jack rubbed his hand over his eyes. "I'm sure you can do something. It doesn't have to be a suite; a room will do."

"I understand, sir, but I don't have any room at all."

"Will you check with the other hotels in the area? I'll stay elsewhere if necessary."

The clerk searched his computer. "I'm sorry, sir, but

the other hotels in the area are also booked. It's Foliage, you understand."

Jack's eyes narrowed, and he glared at the unfortunate clerk. "Yes, I understand it's Foliage, dear God. I just need a room."

"I'm sorry, sir, I can't help you. Miss Morgan got the last room, which was only due to a cancellation."

"I see. Do you have cancellations often?"

"Once every couple of days. Less often during Foliage." He added proudly, "The Country Mill and Inn is a top-rated destination."

The muscles in Jack's jaw twitched. "Yes, I'm sure it is. Please let me have your first cancellation. In the meantime, I'll stay in Miss Morgan's room."

Samantha, who had been enjoying this interplay, was stunned by his cavalier announcement. "What! You will do no such thing!"

Jack looked equally surprised. "Why not? It's only until they get another room. We'll have a rollaway bed brought in."

"We will not. You'll have to get in the car and drive to the next town."

The clerk piped up. "I'm sorry, Miss Morgan, but my computer network is connected to every town for thirty miles. They'll all be booked because of…"

"Foliage!" Jack and Samantha hissed together in exasperation. The clerk shrank back as if they were going to eat him.

Samantha paced the room, unaware elderly patrons eavesdropped on their argument. She'd be damned if he'd stay with her, she thought. He maneuvered his way up here and would have to fend for himself. "Jack, that giant car is out there, all big and empty with its comfy leather bench seats. Why not sleep in it?"

He took her arm, his eyes like cold steel, and dragged her over to a cozy fireplace at one end of the lobby. "Look, Sam, I've come all this way because your father insisted. I was happy to do the paperwork in Dallas. I didn't think getting a room would be a problem. But I won't drive around New Hampshire looking for one that doesn't exist."

His gaze softened. "It will be for a night or two. I won't lay a hand on you, I promise. We'll get them to bring up a rollaway. And I'll string sheets between us, like that guy did in *It Happened One Night*."

How did he know that was her favorite old movie? She loved the sweet romance and innocence of it. But she had never mentioned it to Jack. She smiled at him. His eyes were smoky gray now, no longer angry but warm and hopeful, and a smile played at the edge of his sensuous mouth. Her thoughts came in a torrent. What could one night hurt? Surely, they'd find a room tomorrow. He couldn't sleep in the car; he'd freeze to death. "All right, Jack, only until they get you a room."

He sighed heavily, then led her back to the desk clerk, who looked at Jack with a sort of hero worship. For Samantha it was like Jack had rung the bell at the fair, and she was the prize. She did not like the feeling at all.

The clerk grinned and said, "Yes sir, I'll send a rollaway to two-o-five. And I'll put you down for the next availability."

Sam swore she saw him wink.

Chapter Nine

The room was homey and warm, layered in gingham, Battenburg lace, and handmade patchwork quilts. The honeyed surfaces of the reproduction furniture gleamed in the afternoon light, which slanted off the lake and streamed through the window. Prints of New England folk art hung in rustic frames over the bed and tiny desk. It was an all-together charming room despite its studied newness.

"This is lovely." Samantha breathed as she swept into the room and set her luggage on the long dresser.

"It does seem more comfortable than most hotel rooms. More like a bed and breakfast," Jack agreed and put his luggage beside hers. He shrugged out of his overcoat and navy blazer, then sighed and sat in the floral-covered wing chair anchoring one corner of the room.

Samantha came to stand squarely in front of him. "Don't get so comfortable, Mr. Stone. I believe you have a wall to build."

Jack raised one eyebrow in question. "Right this minute? We just got here. I thought we'd walk through the village and see what we could find for dinner."

That did sound more fun to Samantha, who longed to explore every nook and cranny of the enchanting town. Besides, she was hungry after their long drive. But she didn't want to let Jack off the hook so quickly. "All right, let's go out for a while, but I want us back here in plenty of time to get Housekeeping to send up extra sheets. While we're out, we can buy rope or something."

Jack stood reluctantly. "You're serious about this, aren't you?"

Samantha gave him a mischievous smile, her green eyes flashing. "You bet I am."

He pulled his coat back on and headed for the door. "Lead the way."

Without thinking, Samantha looped her arm through his, and Jack laid his hand on hers. The familiar jolt of electricity passed between them. She looked up quickly to see if Jack had sensed it, too, but he had brought them to an abrupt stop at a plate-glass window and seemed mesmerized by the outside view.

Following his gaze, she gasped in astonishment. The corridor connected the main body of the hotel to a series of separate buildings, housing boutiques and hotel services, in addition to a restaurant and sidewalk cafe. But she hadn't realized the corridor itself was built over the waterfall powering the mill.

It rushed headlong under their feet, tumbling over its stone bed, crashing head over heels in a torrent of white foam until it spilled freely into the roiling blue expanse below, becoming one with the cold, dark waters of the vast lake.

Dusk cloaked the whole scene in gray silk, broken only by the white flashes of the waterfall and the twinkling of thousands of tiny white lights strung artfully through the trees that dotted the landscape surrounding the inn.

Samantha was overwhelmed by the need to be outside, close to the incredible power of Mother Nature summoning water from the rocks. She turned to Jack, who stared silently at the scene below. "Let's go outside. I want to see it up close."

He turned to her, and Samantha thought she had never seen him look so vulnerable, so human. Then, with a little shake of his head, the moment was gone, and his expression unreadable. "Okay, let's go."

A nearby doorway led down a white-painted staircase to a sidewalk that paralleled the waterfall. The noise was deafening. Samantha touched her hand to the water as it gushed by, scooping up the white foam. She blew it away into the crisp October air.

Jack took her wet hand and held it between his, against his chest. The cold was immediately replaced by a rush of heat running up her arm and warming her flushed cheeks. The noise of the waterfall was lost in the drumming of her heart in her ears.

Struggling to control her emotions, Samantha dragged her hand away and shoved it into her pocket. It wouldn't do for Jack to know what his mere touch did to her. Their time in St. Louis together had weakened the last of her defenses against him. If she let him touch her now, she would lose control completely, and her New Year's resolution, hanging by a thread, would be an empty promise, gone as sure as the foam from the waterfall she had blown into the darkening sky.

"What's wrong, Sam?" Jack asked over the roar of the water.

"I'm cold," she answered, hunching her shoulders against the chill air.

"Then, let's find a warm place to eat." He put one arm around her and marched them briskly up the hill to Main Street.

A festival atmosphere pervaded the whole town. Tiny lights festooned the trees that edged the street, the shops, and the restaurants. People everywhere walked quickly in the cold, but outdoors nonetheless, celebrating the season of Foliage.

At the top of the hill, an old brick home had been transformed years earlier into a fine restaurant called Aunt Jane's. Its cozy, intimate dining spaces and several wood-burning fireplaces welcomed Jack and Samantha. A pot of soup simmering on a woodstove beckoned diners to help themselves to its hearty goodness.

Jack settled them into a high-backed booth in a room heavy with brick and wood-beamed ceilings. Candles burning under glass hurricanes cast a mellow glow over the gleaming oak tables.

After a meal of succulent prime rib, accompanied by a rich red wine, they strolled leisurely back to the inn, warmed by the excellent food and lighthearted conversation she had enjoyed throughout the evening. Jack detoured once into an all-night drugstore to buy lightweight rope and clothespins.

Back in the room, he went to work on the makeshift partition, but not without considerable grumbling.

"This has got to be the most ridiculous thing I have ever done. This isn't the Fifties, for heaven's sake!"

Samantha chuckled but held firm. "Sorry, Jack, this was the deal. I appreciate your coming all this way for work, but you can't assume we can share a room."

His head snapped up, eyes flashing like gun metal in the sun. "I didn't plan this, Sam. You know as well as I do there weren't any other rooms."

Samantha didn't want to ruin what had been a perfect evening, so she opted to soothe Jack's ruffled feelings, "Yes, I know this wasn't what you planned. And I appreciate you're being gallant enough to see to my comfort in this situation." She paused, then smiled when he looked at her, his eyes softened to a mere steely gray. "And they said chivalry is dead."

He laughed then and bowed from the waist, making a sweeping gesture at the now completed partition. "Mademoiselle, your virtue is preserved."

Samantha oohed and ahhed as she inspected the makeshift screen. Jack had strung the rope between the beds, from a wall lamp to the television suspended from the ceiling. Sheets obtained from a very curious housekeeping staffer were attached to the rope by the clothespins. The whole thing looked like linen hung out to dry. Samantha was impressed.

"You did a great job. Thank you, Jack." She kissed him quickly on the cheek, then backed away and ducked under the sheet to her side of the room. She emerged a second later. "We do have a problem, though."

"Oh, what's that?"

"Well, the bathroom and closet are on your side. I may have to cross through your territory."

"Mmm, that presents an interesting dilemma," he said, a smile twitching at the corners of his mouth though he tried to appear stern.

"How's that?"

Jack tapped a finger to his lips as he contemplated. "Well, I could extract a heavy toll from you every time you cross over."

Her face flushed, and her heart drummed a little faster. "What kind of toll?"

Jack smiled, his eyebrows raised. "Oh, we'll see, won't we."

Samantha, heart skittering wildly at the danger Jack presented, fought to steel her resolve against him. All the while, she knew she was losing the battle with every passing moment, every sweet, romantic thing he did, every smile, every touch, every word, bringing her closer to the brink. She mustn't fall into the abyss of loving Jack Stone because she knew she would be hurt again.

She lay in bed later, listening to Jack's even breathing as he slept. She had managed to get ready for bed and said a platonic goodnight, avoiding another discussion. Samantha was grateful for that. He had her so confused she needed to think.

Jack didn't love her. He couldn't. His was a fast life. Fast business, fast cars. Women all over the world eager to give themselves to him. To feel the heat of his kiss, the muscled strength of his arms around them, to have him take them on his own fast ride. Samantha wasn't that kind of woman. She knew she seemed provincial, even prudish, to Jack. Only once had she come close to succumbing to the Stone charm—at his hotel in Dallas. Then, he had been the one to stop it. Even he had known she was no match for him.

So why was he here now? To learn more about the business? That could be it. Maybe her father did send him. To solve Joanna's murder? If so, why did he care? He hadn't known her for very long. It could be simple curiosity, of course. But there seemed to be more to it.

Could he be there to spend time with her? It didn't seem likely. But he had been following her for days in Dallas, then insisting on going to Eco-Tek and Bottle Stoppers with her. Bobbie had even said he asked about her appointments almost every day.

Samantha had been flattered, thinking Jack wanted

to be near her, and maybe his actions were the result of genuine feelings, but now, she could think more clearly. Something else was going on here. Jack was up to something, and she would have to find out what.

****

The morning dawned crisp and clear, albeit frosty cold. Samantha knew Jack hadn't slept any better than she had since she'd heard him tossing and turning most of the night, sighing heavily at one point. It didn't help that the creaky rollaway protested loudly every time he moved.

He had gotten up and padded into the bathroom, run the water—getting a drink, she supposed—then slipped back into bed quietly, only to toss and turn again. The sound of the running water made her thirsty, but she didn't dare cross under the sheets to the bathroom since Jack would invariably know she was trespassing on his side of the room.

"Damn," she had muttered to herself, slamming her fist noiselessly into the bed. "This is my room, and I'll get a glass of water if I so choose." But then, she hadn't chosen, lying in the pitch darkness, frustrated, thirsty, and utterly awake until their cell phones announced it was time to get up.

Her fears about dressing in the cramped room and sharing the bath and closet were eased considerably by Jack, who suggested from the other side of the sheet, "Why don't I shower and dress first? Then, I can go to the lobby for a coffee while you dress. When you're ready, you can meet me there, and we'll get breakfast."

Genuinely relieved and grateful, Samantha agreed. "That's a great idea. Thank you."

"No problem. I won't be a minute."

And in no time, he called goodbye to her and left the room whistling. Samantha considered her temporary roommate as she showered and blew her hair dry. Jack had behaved in a chivalrous and gentlemanly fashion, being solicitous to her needs and not pushing her or making a pass at her. So, what was the deal?

Of course, he's luring me into a false sense of security. Then, when my guard is down, he'll take advantage of me like a moth to the flame.

There was enough heat between them to ignite a poor, defenseless moth, she thought and grimaced at her melodramatic metaphor.

Samantha smoothed her hand over her black skirt and picked a microscopic piece of lint from the rust-hued turtleneck sweater. She stepped into spikey black heels and grabbed her camel coat and bag. Taking one last look in the full-length mirror, she scowled at her reflection.

She looked every inch the confident businesswoman—tailored, fashionable, and in control. So why were there flutterings in the pit of her stomach when she thought of Jack? Maybe she was a helpless, stupid moth after all. And was it her imagination, or was it getting hot in there?

****

Green Earth Enterprises was nestled in a birch forest about three miles outside of Meredith, off the same two-lane road by which they had come into town. It was a bland, boxlike structure, windowless from what Samantha could see, except for the area around the entry.

"Now this looks more like a plant," Jack said as he eased the big rental car into a parking spot marked "visitor."

Inside, she and Jack were ushered into an Asian-inspired reception area outside James Hoffman's office. Nothing recycled here, Samantha thought as she looked at the thick, imported rugs, the curated works of art, the richly upholstered seating, and black lacquered tables. Mr. Hoffman must have traveled extensively in Asia, collecting as he went.

The noise of an angry argument drifted through the double doors of Hoffman's office into the reception area. The man's voice, loud, agitated and menacing, assured someone he would not sell, merge, or restructure Green Earth for any amount of money.

Jack glanced at Samantha, his eyebrows raised. "Mr. Hoffman is a little upset, I think."

"Mmm, could be." Samantha leaned in to hear better.

The voice went silent, and the big double doors swung open. A bear of a man stepped through, practically filling the tiny reception room with his massive presence.

Samantha startled at the enormity of him. Jack gasped next to her. Neither were prepared for the sheer size of the man.

"Well, well," he boomed, and Samantha would have sworn the knick-knacks on the bookshelf trembled. "You must be the folks from Dallas."

He shook Jack's hand in what looked like a vise grip that made Samantha nervous to extend hers. She did anyway and was not surprised when he nearly crushed her fingers. She wondered whether the not-so-subtle show of force was meant to let visitors know they were firmly planted in Hoffman's territory, giving him the upper hand in any negotiations to come.

"I'm James Hoffman," he said.

Jack and Samantha introduced themselves, and Hoffman led them through the thick oak doors into an office easily twenty feet square. A bank of windows at the far wall looked onto the parking lot and thick forest beyond. Where the reception area had been decorated with a distinctive and expensive flair for Asia, the office itself was utterly traditional. But, Samantha noted, equally opulent, if not more so.

Heavy hunter-green silk brocade echoing the hues of the plush rug underfoot curtained the windows. To one side, an oversized leather sofa faced a stone fireplace that consumed much of the wall. A crackling blaze warmed the room, its light dancing cheerfully on the crystal decanter and glasses gracing the low table in front of the sofa. On the other side, a well-stocked bar, refrigerator, and microwave were built into the wall. Racks of gleaming glassware hung over the counter and tiny sink. A door next to the bar opened to what looked to Samantha like a full-sized bathroom.

But the most impressive thing in the room, besides Hoffman, was the conference table. The dismembered trunk of what had once been a redwood tree, about four feet in diameter, was topped by a three-inch thick slab of beveled glass. Rising from the center of the table, as if it had sprouted from the tree trunk through the glass, was an enormous arrangement of exotic flowers and greenery crafted of silk and anchored in a giant conch shell.

The island feel of the floral centerpiece seemed out of place in the heavy grandeur of the rest of the room, which, Samantha thought, was the worst display of excess she had ever seen.

"So, Miss Morgan, I was very sorry to hear about Miss Levinson's death. Terrible tragedy. Do they have any idea what happened to her?" Hoffman asked, settling his massive frame into the leather chair behind the mahogany desk.

She disliked the man immediately but forced herself to convey a level of professional friendliness. "No, the authorities are still working on various leads. Nothing has turned up yet." She draped her coat over the back of a leather club chair facing the desk. Attempting to change the subject, she gestured to the table. "I can't help but notice the unusual centerpiece. Not exactly what I would have expected in this room."

The big man stood and walked to the table, where he touched a silken palm frond. "I obtained the shell on a trip to the Keys." He smiled at Samantha, but the expression never reached his eyes. "I had the arrangement made when I got home to commemorate a successful trip."

A sudden unease gripped Samantha's chest. He admitted he'd been to the Keys.

She studied her host as he crossed the room and resumed his seat behind the desk. He was as tall as her father but far heavier and solid as a maple tree. His beady eyes shifted from being shrewd and calculating one minute to congenial and warm the next. Carefully styled brown hair, perfectly manicured nails, highly polished wingtips, and an exquisitely tailored suit completed the picture of a man who had it all and enjoyed flaunting all he had.

Samantha cast a side-long glance at Jack. He sat in the chair next to hers, elbows on the chair arms, fingertips together, tapping his narrowed lips.

He seemed about to speak when Hoffman abruptly stood and bellowed, "Well, let's see the plant, shall we?

I'm quite proud of this operation—cutting edge, technologically speaking. We get the fabric from a manufacturer in North Carolina and then make all the garments in this facility. When we finish touring the plant, I'll take you to the showroom, where you can view our finished line. I'm sure you'll find several items you like, Miss Morgan."

He smiled warmly and placed his big hand on her back, gently guiding her through the office door he held open for them both. Samantha shivered as she left the stifling warmth of the office for the cool air in the reception area.

The high-tech array of equipment and machines in the plant impressed her. A handful of people worked on selected machines, cutting, sewing, and finishing sweatshirts, jackets, hats, and gloves. Several other workers maneuvered long aluminum racks groaning under the weight of hundreds of garments in plastic bags.

Jack, who hadn't spoken, said, "I'm impressed by the level of technical advances I'm seeing here. It looks like you've replaced several employees with robotic manufacturing machines."

Samantha was surprised at Jack's insightful question. She had thought the same thing. *So, he is paying attention. Maybe he cares about this job after all.*

Hoffman, too, seemed pleased at Jack's interest. "Right. Right. We've found the quality doesn't suffer, and after the initial investment, the bottom line doesn't either." He clapped Jack on the back. "That's what it's all about, eh, Stone?"

Jack glanced at Samantha, an odd grimace on his face.

"Well, it's important to balance quality, value, and

company ethics to be sure," she ventured.

Hoffman turned to her and leaned in a little. "I'm sure you'll find, Miss Morgan, Green Earth prides itself on modeling excellence in everything we do." He straightened and gestured down the hallway. "Let's take a look at the product."

In the small display space, several mannequins wore fleecy sweaters, jackets, hats, and gloves. There were stacks of colorful children's clothes, pants, and tops. Samantha's cursory examination confirmed the quality was excellent, and the garments exceeded her expectations.

She didn't have to like James Hoffman to concede his company produced a fine product. Several would be ideal for the next season. "Mr. Hoffman, we'd like to discuss including some of your products in our next line. There are details to be ironed out, of course, but we're pleased by what we've seen."

"Allow me to take you to dinner, and we'll discuss nuts and bolts. I know a wonderful old place. It's a converted barn out in the country. They serve great steaks. I might even brag they would rival Texas." He smiled warmly at Samantha, eyes twinkling.

He could be quite charming, she thought warily. It would be easy to be swayed by this big bear of a man, oozing money and charm. She wondered if that had happened to Joanna, and it was James Hoffman she had been seeing in New Hampshire, and it was he who met her in Key West, and it was he who killed her.

She glanced at Jack for confirmation about dinner and was startled by the glint of steel in his gray eyes. It seemed Hoffman had taken neither of them in.

Pasting a smile on her face, she turned back to

Hoffman. "We'd love to meet you. Text us the address."

"Nonsense, I'll send a car. Seven o'clock."

Jack managed a charming smile. "Thank you. We'll be looking forward to that steak." He ushered Samantha out of the building and into the afternoon sun.

****

Back at the hotel, she and Jack had time before dinner to debrief about their trip to Green Earth.

Jack paced around the room, voicing what Samantha had been thinking. "I don't like that guy. He's a crook. He looks like a crook, and he acts like a crook. It wouldn't surprise me if he murdered Joanna."

"I was thinking the same thing. He's so…slimy. But what about S.L.? Those aren't his initials. Of course, we didn't meet anyone else."

Jack stopped pacing and collapsed in the chair. "We may have to admit Joanna's murder had nothing to do with R.L. Morgan."

"You don't believe that for a minute. What about the gunshot and the car bomb? You think those were coincidences?"

Jack sighed and ran his hand through his hair. "No, no, I don't." He got up and began pacing again. "And there's something funny going on at Green Earth. I'm trying to put my finger on it."

Samantha squared her shoulders and put her hands on her hips. "I totally agree. We have to go back tomorrow."

"Good idea. We need to see their complete operation. I don't think we saw the whole thing. What about design…incoming materials…fitting…shipping?"

"You're right. We saw all that at Bottle Stoppers and Eco-Tek."

Jack shook his head. "I don't know if we can split up like we did at Bottle Stoppers. I don't think Hoffman will let either one of us out of his sight for a minute."

"No, he loves having control, doesn't he?"

Jack massaged his hand. "He nearly broke my hand. There was no mistaking the message I was in his territory, and he was the Alpha male."

Samantha laughed. "I know what you mean. I got the feeling he could eat me alive."

Jack frowned, stopped pacing, and put his hands on Samantha's shoulders. "Look, be careful around this guy. Don't give him any slack."

"What do you mean?"

"If he didn't kill Joanna, then, he probably knows who did. And it was probably at his bidding. He won't hesitate to do it again." He dropped his hands from her shoulders and cupped her face, lifting her chin to meet his gaze. "I don't want anything to happen to you."

She looked into his cool, gray eyes, heavy with an emotion she couldn't read. "I promise I'll be careful."

****

Later that evening, Green Earth's limousine picked Jack and Samantha up and whisked them through the darkening countryside. Samantha could make out the ancient stone fences edging fields and yards, standing guard over centuries-old houses and farms, protecting a rich heritage Samantha yearned to know more about.

She was drawn to this place as if a distant part of her belonged to the past, and the past was here. She felt it in the desolate cries of the loons on the lake, the fiery colors of the leaves on the trees, and the simple structures that hearkened back to a time gone by. Sinking into the leather-covered seats, she thought she would have to return to New Hampshire, Lake Winnipesaukee, and Meredith to discover the siren song calling her here.

She looked away from the window to Jack, who gazed at her longingly. He glanced away and stared out his own window. "It's wonderful here, isn't it? Not merely the trees but the whole atmosphere. It's like time stood still somehow."

"That's exactly what it's like," Samantha agreed, glad to discover Jack had the same feelings she had.

Before they could discuss it further, the driver swung the long car onto the gravel drive and up to the heavy, sliding wooden doors of a cavernous barn that had been transformed into what appeared to be a trendy steak house.

Inside they were met by the garrulous James Hoffman, who had already had a couple of Scotch and sodas, judging by the discarded glasses and his gruff instructions to the waiter to bring another.

She and Jack sat on a bench under a giant wagon wheel at a rough-hewn table. Hoffman sat across from them. Antique farming implements were everywhere, including a full-sized plow harnessed to a team of plaster horses. Several young children climbed on them with noisy abandon.

To their left, two beefy men sat quietly eating and, Samantha noticed, not drinking. They perused the room like their heads were on swivels, obviously on alert for any occurrence. Hoffman's bodyguards, Samantha decided. But she dismissed their presence and tried to enjoy dinner.

Once steaks had been ordered and a round of drinks procured, Samantha commented, "This place is a good example of that old New England proverb, 'use it up, wear it out, make it do, or do without.' Nothing seems to be thrown away up here. Someone turns it into a restaurant, hotel, or shop."

"I suppose so. These people are a thrifty lot, and nothing goes to waste. I admire that. It's sound business practice," Hoffman replied, draining his glass.

"Tell me, Mr. Hoffman," Jack said. "Making clothing from recycled water bottles seems an unusual direction for a man of your tastes. How did you end up in this business?"

"I took the company over in a buy-out. The man who started Green Earth was one of those tree-hugging environmentalists—lots of good intentions, no head for business. I saw a cutting-edge trend. I see the future, Stone. And I'm a businessman. As you are."

Jack stiffened beside her. While she hadn't expected Hoffman's motives to be as pure as the driven snow, she would have preferred he actually believed in the product, not just the profit. But, before she could say anything, the waitress placed huge platters of sizzling steaks and baked potatoes in front of them, and the remainder of the evening was spent enjoying the succulent meal and their host's entertaining stories of his travels and business dealings.

Before dessert was served, Hoffman regaled her and Jack with an uproarious recounting of his big-game safari trip to Africa and how a gnu sporting enormous horns chased them.

"We shot him a couple of times, but he just kept charging. Stupid beast." He shook his head. "He kept butting our vehicle, trying to leap inside." Hoffman roared with laughter and slapped Jack on the back. "I got him in the end, though, and now that gnu's horns are on the wall in my study."

Samantha's heart lurched at the thought. While she understood hunting and fishing for both sport and food, she hated that Hoffman shot such an intriguing animal.

Jack said, "So, even if the gnu's perseverance didn't pay off, yours did." It didn't sound like a compliment.

Hoffman leaned over the table, close enough for Samantha to smell the whiskey on his breath. "I always get what I want."

Before he deposited them in the limousine for the trip to the inn, Hoffman arranged to meet the next day and finalize the selections for the product line. Samantha thanked him for the delicious dinner. Jack conceded the steak came close to the perfection of Texas beef.

Hoffman laughed out loud. "Well, I know this isn't the most luxurious place to eat. It's noisy and smells like sawdust. But you can't find a better steak anywhere in New England. So, I put up with the bratty kids and concentrate on the food. Glad you liked it. I'll see you tomorrow."

The car door slammed shut, and Jack leaned back on the seat. "What an arrogant jerk." He looked intently at Samantha. "Sam, I know his stuff looks good, but are you sure you want to do business with this guy? I have a bad feeling about him."

"I know, I don't like him either. But you're right. His merchandise is great and exactly what we've been looking for. Plus, I'm still not convinced he wasn't involved in Joanna's murder." She looked into Jack's worried eyes. "You know what they say. Keep your enemies close."

"All right, we'll do more sleuthing tomorrow, but I'm telling you, something isn't right."

Chapter Ten

Samantha's side of the room featured a picture window facing the lake. She opened the drapes and stood looking out over the dark expanse bisected by a glittering trail of moonlight. The serenity comforted her, calming her jangling nerves, set on edge, no doubt, by the overly genial James Hoffman. And, Samantha realized, by two days of close proximity to Jack.

She could hear him in the bathroom, humming a show tune in the shower.

He's certainly less jittery than I am.

She was disconcerted by the effect he had on her. She pictured him naked, under the running water, jet-black hair slicked back, well-honed body glistening wet, covered in soapsuds. She could almost feel his warm, damp skin under her fingertips and smell his clean scent.

Good heavens, girl, get hold of yourself, or you'll rush into the bathroom and attack the poor man. She laughed at her own foolishness. Picking up the discarded bestseller she had started on the plane, she found her mind wandering back to the man in the shower.

He quit singing and came out of the bathroom. "It's all yours, Sam."

She pushed open the sheet. He stood by the bed on the other side of the room. Wearing only a towel wrapped casually around his waist, he was as she had pictured him, sans soapsuds. His tan skin beaded in tiny

145

droplets of water the towel had failed to reach…a towel that did little to obscure his complete maleness.

Her breath caught in her throat, and her heart began to race. Not so much from the sight of him as from embarrassment at what she had been thinking. He grinned at her as if, once again, he had read her mind.

She hurriedly grabbed her nightshirt and brushed past, not daring to look at him for fear he would see the incriminating blush burning her face. Once in the bathroom, she shut the door and leaned against it until her breathing returned to normal.

Why, oh why, had he come to New Hampshire? She didn't know how long she could keep an emotional distance from this man who continued to chip away at her defensive wall. A part of her wanted him here, but another, more rational part was terrified of being near him, terrified of what it would mean if he knew the power he had over her.

Jack wasn't the kind of man she wanted—a solid, stable man, someone who would love her and love the simple things as she did. Someone who would appreciate the things she had discovered here in New Hampshire: history, heritage, tradition. They were the same things she had hoped to find in Williamsburg that ill-fated Christmas and the same things that told her to cherish and protect the earth.

Jack was a modern man, wasn't he? He wouldn't be content to settle down and enjoy the simple pleasures in life. Certainly not a life that included someone as mundane and ordinary as she.

So why was he here? Why had he followed her to New Hampshire? Why the chivalrous treatment, the romantic dinner? Did Jack see something special in her?

Had she touched a part of him he kept hidden from the world? That same aspect of his personality that wanted a warm and inviting home furnished in antiques, plants, and cats?

Jack was a mystery, Samantha thought as she adjusted the shower knobs and stepped under the invigorating stream of hot water, letting its pulsating warmth wash over her. The day's tension flowed from her shoulders and neck under the liquid massage. Thoughts of Jack and his motives eased from her mind and down the drain, and she was left mentally holding only the picture of him standing naked and damp in the room, invitingly clad in a hotel towel.

Samantha fully expected the room to be dark and Jack to be well on his way to sleep by the time she toweled her hair dry and slipped out of the bathroom. She was grateful she had brought the comfy, oversized football jersey to sleep in. It wasn't her habit to sleep in frilly, lacy gowns, and she hadn't even brought a robe since she was hardly planning to share her accommodations with a virile male co-worker.

To her surprise, that same co-worker lounged on his bed, lights fully on, watching a late-night talk show. He had managed to discard the towel, but the pajama bottoms he wore did little to calm Samantha's racing pulse. He was propped up against the pillows, the sculpted muscles of his chest smooth and brown, with an outcropping of curling black hair. Samantha's fingers twitched, longing to reach out and touch him.

He grinned at her and patted the bed next to him. "Come here and watch. A guy is coming on who's got a new tell-all about the president."

She hesitated, too aware of her own spiraling need

to be close to him, too aware that a single touch, a single kiss, might strip away the last brick of her wall. And she was too aware that whether Jack was right for her no longer mattered; she loved his company, trusted his judgment, and believed his sincerity. She could fight it in intellectual terms, but her body and her heart knew the truth. She loved Jack Stone.

And she must stay away from him.

"No, my side—your side, remember," she said, gesturing to her bed beyond the flimsy cotton wall. "I'm exhausted. I'm going to sleep. Keep watching your show. It won't bother me."

Jack stood and faced her between the beds. "Look, Sam, we're both adults here. Surely, we can watch a little television without things ending up…awkward."

A delicious mental picture threatened Samantha's resolve, but she steeled herself against it, employing feigned formality. "I'm not afraid of watching TV in your company, Jack. I simply am tired and want to go to sleep."

He moved a step closer. His warm breath whispered across her temple. She stared at the drawstring on his pants, then thought better of it and jerked her head up to meet his flinty gaze. He said, "Then I guess you won't mind a goodnight kiss."

Her voice squeaked, "Of course not. Don't be silly." She closed her eyes and tilted her head to meet his.

He brushed a gentle kiss across her lips, then, her eyes still closed and mouth parted, he plopped back down on the bed…"Goodnight, Sam."

Her eyes snapped open. A triumphant smirk covered his beautiful face. Without speaking, she yanked the sheet-divider closed and threw herself on the bed.

Humiliation and fury washed over her in alternate waves, and she pounded the pillow into submission, then crammed it behind her head.

She could see the TV from where she sat as easily as Jack could. She knew she'd never sleep as long as he was awake on the other side of the makeshift wall. She might as well watch. And listen.

A parade of predictable jokes, a celebrity or two, and an obscure musical guest followed, but later, Samantha couldn't remember any of them. She was only aware of Jack's nearness and every sound he made.

He scrunched the pillow behind his head and slurped a sip of water. He kicked the covers off with an exasperated sigh. Samantha recreated his image in her mind: the well-hewn head and splendid crown of shining black hair, the dusting of the same dark hair on his arms, the rise and fall of his chest as he breathed, the washboard stomach that contracted when he moved, slender hips, lean, powerful legs. She shifted uncomfortably.

There was only silence from the other side of the curtain when the show ended. The next show started featuring a single guest and call-ins from around the country. Samantha was no more interested than before and only strained to hear Jack's movements, which seemed to have stopped.

She thought he must have fallen asleep, knowing it would be hours before she could do the same and trying to figure out how to turn the set off without waking him.

"Sam?"

She jumped. "Yes?"

"How long do you think we should go on this way? You over there and me over here? Slowly going crazy, I might add, thinking about you in that damned football jersey."

She smiled. Little did he know what she had been thinking about him. But she couldn't let him know. So, she said as lightly as possible, "Oh, Jack, I'm sure you'll survive. We'll be going home the day after tomorrow."

The sheets rustled from the other side of the curtain.

"Do you mean to tell me this ridiculous arrangement doesn't bother you at all?"

She lied quickly—too quickly, probably, "No, not at all."

"Well, it's bothering the hell out of me!"

The makeshift wall between them jerked once, and then one of the sheets fluttered to the carpet, leaving the remaining sheet dangling precariously by a single clothespin. Jack stood there, towering over her, his hands balled at his sides, eyes as stormy as thunder clouds.

Samantha gasped and drew the covers up under her chin.

Jack kneeled on the bed and slowly stripped the sheet and thin blanket away. "If you don't want this, tell me now. I'll stop." He stared at her, molten steel from under hooded lids.

She didn't try to stop him but held her breath, unable to will her body to move away. "Sam, tell me you don't want me the way I want you. That you don't think about us night and day."

"I've tried to stay away from you, Jack. I have, but I want you, too."

The world seemed to stop turning. Jack lowered his head, and his lips warmed hers, light, tentative almost, savoring every morsel. Slowly, so slowly, his tongue urged her teeth apart, then began a lazy ransacking of the inner recesses of her mouth. When he had his fill, he moved on to sample her neck, earlobe, eyelid, and temple as if he would gladly nibble her up in small portions.

The silent assault hypnotized Samantha. Every place he kissed tingled; every other place screamed for its turn. The feel of his lips on her skin, his clean soap smell, and the sound of her own shallow breathing mesmerized her.

He shifted her so she faced him, almost in his lap, cradled in his arm. She sighed contentedly and snuggled closer to him, her arms twining around his neck.

"Jack." It wasn't a question or request, but a statement, as if saying his name aloud would help to maintain the tenuous bond between them.

"I'm here," he said, reading her thoughts and capturing her mouth again.

Time moved quickly then. Her tongue found his and started a game of thrust and parry. Claiming victory, she seized a long, searching kiss as her prize. Jack responded with demands of his own. The kiss deepened until Samantha could scarcely breathe, and she wondered fleetingly what it would be like to die in his arms.

She broke the kiss long enough to run her fingertips over his jaw, down his throat to his shoulder. There was a scar there, and she traced it with her lips, almost as if she could heal him. He growled and pulled her back to him, capturing her mouth again.

A new addition to the game began as Jack's hands kneaded her shoulders, caressed her back, and trailed the length of her arm, then up to cup one round breast, teasing the nipple through the thin cotton.

Samantha's low moan was his reward, and he upped the ante. One deft hand slid under the shirt, quickly casting it aside. Flesh met flesh, and where it touched, a fire burned. His mouth never left hers, but his hands continued to roam, first down the ravine of her spine, around one side of her bottom, still clad in silky panties, then retraced his earlier steps, to end stroking one breast, then the other.

This kind of lovemaking was new to Samantha. Gary had made sex a perfunctory activity—precise and sterile—never with the lights on, in front of the television. Never with his hand—oh, God—what Jack was doing with his hands!

He had eased down her panties, then slid the obstructive garment over her feet and dropped it over the edge of the bed. Samantha gasped, then sighed, then gasped again as Jack touched the soft skin of her thighs, nudging her legs apart, and moved his fingers into the moist, throbbing heart of her growing need for him.

She dug her hands into the muscles of his back, urging him even closer.

He took one hardened nipple in his mouth and suckled it, his teeth nipping the sensitized peak until Samantha thought she couldn't feel anything more wonderful than this.

He fumbled for the remote, switched off the television, and turned off the overhead light, leaving one lamp glowing. He turned back to Samantha, eyes smoky with desire. His gaze traveled slowly over her, his burning hunger searing her tender flesh. "Sam, you're beautiful, absolutely beautiful."

He reached for the drawstring at the waist of his pajama bottoms, bulging now with his need for her. She stilled his hands with her trembling fingers. "Let me," she said and undid the knot, tugging the soft fabric over his hips.

It was her turn to stare. He was magnificent and not a little frightening. She wasn't prepared for the perfectly sculpted male animal stretched out beside her.

He pulled her down to lie next to him, unaware of the effect he had on her, then began again his patient, deliberate assault on her senses.

He covered every inch of her smooth skin with kisses, starting at her toes and working his way up. He did with his tongue what he had done earlier with his fingers until she writhed in exquisite torture, moaning his name.

At last, when Samantha had lost all sense of anything but the feel of Jack's hands igniting her skin, his breath fanning the fire, knowing any moment she would burst into flames, he entered her. Gently, tenderly, he whispered sweet nonsense in her ear.

She wrapped her legs around him, urging him closer still. Then he began the rhythmic friction that set them both afire, a conflagration of souls and bodies, minds and hearts. And in an instant, all the doubts in Samantha's mind burned to the ground, leaving only the ashes blown away by Jack's cooling breath, ruffling her hair as she lay spent in his arms.

Samantha nestled in Jack's embrace under the thick comforter. He snored softly, but she couldn't sleep. Her skin still tingled from his touch, her lips were swollen from his kisses, and her psyche reeled from the thoughts careening through her mind.

What had she done? Jack had finally broken through her wall of resolve and smashed all her defenses to dust. She could only pray he was a man of integrity and honor—someone who wouldn't lie to her or betray her trust.

She fell into a heavy, dreamless sleep.

****

I'm a dead man.

Jack awoke before dawn, aware of the weight of Sam's arm across his chest. The comfort of it did little to assuage the guilt and dread consuming him. He'd let his feelings for Sam cloud his judgment and completely overpower his good sense. What was he thinking? He had done the one thing Vince had demanded he not do. Get involved with a client.

Well, he was involved all right. Right down to the throbbing part of him that even now wanted nothing more than to wake Sam up and ravish her again.

Had he lost his mind? Vince was going to kill him. And then fire him.

And what about R.L? Not even his military training would save him from the fate awaiting him if R.L. found out he'd slept with his daughter…the woman he vowed to protect. The huge bear would tear him limb from limb.

Not to mention the fact that all the killing, firing, and maiming to come will be for nothing when Sam finds out I've been lying to her all this time.

He groaned aloud and Sam stirred slightly, then made a little sighing noise and snuggled closer to him.

He had to tell her the truth and it had to be soon. He couldn't risk her finding out from Jordan or the company grapevine. Vince and R.L. would have to wait 'til later.

If the plan he'd been formulating worked, it wouldn't matter anyway. Everything would be okay.

He glanced out the window. The rosy dawn peeked through the curtains. It would be light soon.

He turned toward Sam, careful not to wake her, and

buried his face in her hair, breathing in her scent. It was one of the things he'd remember if his plan went awry.

****

Well after the sun was up, Jack made coffee in the room and brought her a cup.

She took a sip, grimaced, and laughed. "This is truly terrible."

He set his cup down. "I know. Let's go downstairs. The coffee is better, and I need nourishment." He dragged her out of bed and shooed her into the bathroom, patting her bare bottom.

Earlier, she had enjoyed an entirely different form of nourishment from him, savoring him in ways she hadn't explored the night before.

Jack seemed genuinely to care about her and couldn't have been more attentive to her needs. He was romantic and sweet, waking her with kisses and whispered endearments, caresses and cuddling. Indeed, he was no Gary, as he had sworn.

Over breakfast in the hotel dining room, Samantha delighted in a breathtaking view of the waterfall through two-story windows. Afterward the subject turned to business, and she said, "We need to get ready for our visit to Green Earth today."

Jack said, "Right. I've been thinking, and I know what's been bothering me—the plant's too small."

"What do you mean, too small?" she asked, munching a cream-cheese laden bagel.

"Doesn't it seem small to you? Considering the volume of merchandise they claim to produce there?"

Samantha chewed thoughtfully. "You may be right. Eco-Tek has a bigger facility than Green Earth, but they don't produce nearly the volume Green Earth says it does."

"We've only seen one facility. Maybe they have another plant somewhere."

"I don't think so. Joanna didn't say much in her notes, but she was clear this was their only location."

"Mmm, are they fudging on their reported volume? They could want R.L. Morgan's business badly enough to lie about production."

"Well, we need to find out because if they can't fill the order, we've got customers who'll be mad at us on the other end."

"We'll ask Hoffman a few pertinent questions when we get there," Jack said. He paused and took Samantha's hand, turning it over in his own, then kissed the palm tenderly. A familiar jolt of electricity shot up her arm. "There's something I have to do in town. It'll take about an hour. Do you want to come with me?"

"What are you up to, Jack? Where are you going?"

"Uh-huh. It's a surprise. I'll tell you later." He signaled the waiter for the check.

They left the restaurant and stepped into the blinking sunlight.

The day was crisp and cool, and Samantha buttoned her jacket. "Do you mind if we walk?"

"No, not at all." He raised an eyebrow.

"I want to explore the nooks and crannies of this cute little town." She walked up the hill, with Jack close behind, and turned onto the narrow main street, strolling idly, stopping to look in shop windows. "What a nice change from the mall," she said, more to herself than to Jack. Across the street was a quaint antiques store where she had seen an ancient ship's wheel in the window. Curious, she said, "Ooh, come on. I want to go over there."

He rolled his eyes. "Sure, you know I can't deny you anything."

She stepped off the curb. A car careened toward her, not slowing. Jack jerked her backward, and they tripped over the curb, sprawling onto the sidewalk. The car whooshed past, spraying them in muddy water.

Jack jumped to his feet and ran into the street, looking for the vehicle. He hurried back to Samantha, who struggled to get up.

"Are you okay?" He searched her face, smoothing her hair and holding her to him.

She clutched his jacket, shaking. "I think so. Did you see the car?"

"No, it disappeared around the corner. Late model, blue sedan. I didn't get the plates."

A woman rushed over. "Good Lord, I thought he was going to hit you for sure. I was inside the shop, and you couldn't hear me yelling at you. But I saw him coming. Hell-bent on hitting you, it looked to me." She pointed to Samantha's leg. "That's a nasty cut. Come in the store. We'll put something on it."

Samantha looked down at the gash on her leg. It was about two inches long and bleeding badly. She must have hit the mailbox next to the curb when she and Jack fell.

Jack helped her into the nearby store—a pharmacy, as luck would have it.

"Do you work here?" Jack asked.

The woman laughed. "I have to. It belongs to me." She dabbed a wet cloth around the wound and then applied a thick layer of ointment.

"The pharmacy is yours?" Samantha asked.

"Yep. Been in my family for years." She wrapped

Samantha's leg in layers of gauze, then secured the bandage with tape. "It's not deep, and I think I cleaned it well enough. It'll be sore, and you might have a scar, but I don't think it needs stitches."

"That's a professional-looking job," Samantha commented.

The woman beamed. "Thought years ago I might go into medicine, but then Dad died, and I took over the store. It's the next best thing if you want to help people. I bet I give out as much medical advice as any doctor. All free, of course." She laughed, her wrinkled face crinkling even more.

"Thank you very much, Mrs...."

"It's Emma, honey. Glad I was here." She smiled warmly and squeezed Samantha's hand.

Samantha and Jack left the store and hurried back to the inn, keeping a close eye on the traffic, sparse as it was that time of day. Back at the hotel, they were able to change clothes. Samantha took care not to disturb Emma's expert bandage.

Hoping to add a little levity to the situation, she modeled the bandage as if it were a new pair of shoes. "Very nice work, don't you think? It should be all the rage in Dallas."

"Very funny, Sam." His face was like thunder, and he sounded serious, almost angry. Clearly, he didn't think it was funny at all.

"What's wrong, Jack? It was an accident. The guy probably never saw us."

He stared at her. "Sam, think. It was no accident. Someone tried to kill you. Again."

Samantha remembered the car and the man at the wheel, coming steadily for them. "You're right, he barreled straight toward us. I thought he was out of control at the time, but now, it's almost as if it were on purpose."

Jack slammed his fist on the dresser.

She crossed the room and kissed him lightly, quickly. "It's okay, Jack. We're okay. You were there this time. You saved me."

He gathered her close in a very tight, very protective embrace and whispered in her ear, "Sam, I won't ever let anything happen to you. I love you, and I don't want to lose you."

She tilted her head and looked into his smoky gray eyes. Her fingers stroked his ebony hair, touched his ear, his cheek, his lips. "I love you, Jack. I'll try not to get lost," she murmured.

She kissed him to seal their bargain—a kiss that spoke of a future to be shared.

Then the kiss deepened, a yearning expressed and confirmed, a question asked and answered, a longing unspoken but made known. It wasn't enough to say the words aloud. A closer bond, a stronger vow, was needed.

Samantha sighed as Jack unbuttoned her blouse and laid it aside. His finger traced the top of the lacy bra she wore underneath. She shivered when his touch went deeper beneath the thin fabric, taunting the sensitive flesh into firm peaks.

"Jack," she moaned, loosening his tie. "Do we have time for this? We have to be at Green Earth in an hour."

"This, sweetheart, is the most important thing on my agenda for the day," he said, plucking the bra away in one swift motion and weighing the soft mounds of her breasts in each hand. He kissed each one thoroughly, then backed her up to the bed, unbuttoning his shirt as he went.

She unzipped his pants and tentatively touched the velvety softness beneath the briefs he wore. Jack moaned, a low, guttural sound akin to a growl. He slid the unnecessary garments to the floor as Samantha undid her skirt and let it fall. She allowed him to remove her panties, taking special care of her injured leg before she lay back on the bed.

Jack straddled her legs. He claimed her eager mouth while his hand found its place between her soft thighs, coaxing her to the edge of release, then slowing its rhythmic motion until her ragged breathing calmed.

He reached for a condom, but she held out her hand. "Let me," she said, wanting to give back the pleasure he had given her. He lay back on the bed, one arm thrown over his eyes.

Samantha touched him gingerly at first, then became fascinated by the incredible softness of his skin, the rough textured curly hair, and his velvet-over-iron firmness, and she gained confidence. Her fingers caressed and fondled him until his hips writhed and his hand gripped the sheet.

"Now, Sam," he commanded in a voice barely audible.

She slipped the condom over the throbbing shaft. He flipped her to her back and moved swiftly between her legs, capturing her mouth once again, whispering against her lips, "Come with me now, sweetheart."

She gave in to the rhythm of the ancient dance.

Chapter Eleven

The tires of the rental car crunched the gravel in Green Earth Enterprises' parking lot, then came to a stop. Samantha and Jack sat for a few minutes, studying the plant.

"I don't see any other buildings," Samantha observed.

"I don't either. And it looks like what we saw inside is all there is of this one building. No annexes or additional wings. Only one big box."

"This is a regular business day, right? They should be at full production. Take note of the number of employees. Yesterday, they seemed to have only a skeleton crew."

"I noticed that, too. But they did have a lot of those huge racks of finished garments."

"Good quality, too. You know, as much as I dislike Hoffman and as weird as this operation seems, I would love to carry their merchandise."

"Well, let's check it out a little closer," Jack said, opening his car door.

Inside, she was surprised to be greeted not by James Hoffman but by a wiry little man with a pencil-thin mustache. "Elgin Lenhart," he said, offering his hand to Jack, then Samantha. "Mr. Hoffman had an emergency meeting this morning and asked if I would answer any further questions you may have."

Elgin Lenhart was affable, friendly, and eager to please. Samantha liked him immediately. "We'd like to see the plant again if you don't mind. We're eager to ensure all the environmental sensitivity claims are valid."

"Certainly, right this way." He led them down a hallway she knew from the day before housed the offices of the business operation—finance, personnel, and marketing. He stopped at a phone on the wall at the end of the hallway, dialed a few numbers, and spoke briefly, "Elgin, here. I'm bringing the folks from R.L. Morgan in." He replaced the receiver and led them through the double doors, which seemed to open magically into the plant.

Since the offices were on the left side and back of the box, the plant occupied space on the front and right side. Once again, she saw the entire operation, from receiving the fabric from the plant in North Carolina to cutting, sewing, and finishing. She saw original designs draped on forms and finished garments sized on live models. And she saw no more people working than she had the day before.

Jack saw it, too. "Mr. Lenhart, are you at full production now?" he asked when the tour ended, and they were back in the reception area.

"Pretty much. It does pick up more in late spring as we're trying to get out the fall line to the retailers. But we like to keep our employees working year-round; it creates loyalty and improves production, as you know."

"And this is your only facility? Everything is made here? Except the fabric, of course."

"Yes, we have more quality control if we manufacture everything here. We're not a huge operation, Miss Morgan, but you'll find we're quite efficient and always meet our shipping deadlines."

"Yes, that's what I've heard. You have a good reputation for quality and service, Mr. Lenhart. That's why R.L. Morgan is interested in doing business with you. I'll have my admin email you the contract for the items we want to carry."

"I'll be waiting to hear from you, Miss Morgan. Mr. Stone, thank you both for coming to Meredith. I hope you've enjoyed your stay."

"It's been very nice, thank you. We'll be in touch," Jack said as he and Samantha moved through the front doors toward the parking lot.

Standing beside the car, Samantha fished in her purse for her sunglasses. A piece of paper, she wasn't sure what it was, fluttered out and across the parking lot. Carried by the wind, it led her on a merry chase around the corner of the building. She stomped one high heel on it and bent to retrieve it. "Only a gasoline receipt!" she muttered.

She looked up to see several men unloading long racks of finished and bagged garments from a truck marked FISH into the plant area of the building. Jack came up behind her in time to watch the processional of racks—about ten in all. Samantha estimated they carried close to a thousand garments.

Suddenly, one of the men spied them at the corner of the building. He gestured to another who approached them. He was burly and unshaven, wearing a plaid flannel shirt.

"This is a restricted area. You'll have to leave."

"Certainly. I was chasing a piece of paper the wind carried over here," Samantha offered.

They hurried back to the car while the burly man watched until they rolled out of the driveway and into the birch trees.

"Good grief! Who was that?" Samantha giggled, breathless, still clutching the errant receipt.

"Never mind him. Did you see what they were doing?"

"Yes! Why would they unload finished garments into a plant where those same garments are supposedly being made?"

"They wouldn't unless the garments—or most of them from the looks of it—are being made elsewhere and brought to this location for shipping."

"Which means Hoffman and Lenhart were lying. Why would they do that? We wouldn't care if they had a dozen plants as long as we can visit them, and they can fill the order."

"They wouldn't have any reason to lie to us unless they have something else to hide. But what?"

Samantha chewed on her fingernail. "Maybe they aren't living up to their environmental claims. Maybe the fabric isn't made of recycled PET."

"That wouldn't explain them trucking in finished garments from someplace else."

"True. It must be something else. They must have another plant they don't want us to know about."

"No, wait." Jack pulled the car to the side of the narrow road and stopped. He turned to Samantha, eyes glinting like gunmetal. "I'll bet you anything, it's the government they're keeping secrets from, too. Probably tax evasion. Whatever, you can bet it's illegal."

"Jack," Samantha exclaimed, her heart racing. "Do you think Joanna found out what Hoffman was doing?

Do you think he killed her to keep her quiet?"

"Yeah, Sam," he answered slowly. "I think that's exactly what happened."

****

That afternoon, Jack left Sam in the room and went to run the errand which had been interrupted when the car careened into them. "Do not under any circumstances let anyone in. I don't care who it is."

Samantha promised and spent the time napping. When Jack returned an hour later, he kissed her awake and offered her a warm chocolate chip cookie.

He had ordered coffee, and she spent the rest of the afternoon quietly enjoying his company.

Later, Samantha sat by the window in their room at the inn, looking at the lake. "Do you suppose Joanna knew he knew she knew?"

Jack shook his head and chuckled. "Run that by me again?"

"Do you think Joanna knew Hoffman suspected she had found him out?"

"I don't know, why?"

"I was thinking about her. She was in danger, but she didn't seem to know it. She went snorkeling that day, either alone or with someone she knew and had arranged to meet. That doesn't sound like someone who was expecting to be killed."

"No, it doesn't, so either she met him thinking he didn't know she was onto him—" Jack sat down in the chair facing her. "—Or she innocently met a mystery man, and he killed her."

"Well, she was probably killed by someone she trusted. We know she was dating someone from New Hampshire. Someone she was trying to keep secret from other employees." She propped her elbows on the table and rested her chin in her hands.

"It stands to reason it was Hoffman."

"That would explain a lot. She wouldn't have wanted anyone to know she was dating a vendor. Conflict of interest."

Jack got up and paced the room. "Plus, we know from the ugly flower arrangement he was in the Keys recently."

"I don't know. I can't picture Hoffman snorkeling. He'd get his wingtips all wet."

Jack laughed. "And we still haven't addressed the initials S.L., either."

"Maybe they stood for something else, not a name."

Jack scratched his head. "Sure, that's possible."

Samantha said, "Well, Joanna must have stumbled onto *something*. Or they thought she had."

"Or she put two and two together like we did and began to investigate on her own. Maybe she got too close to the truth for Hoffman's comfort." Jack stared out the window. "Like they think you have."

"They must think I know what Joanna knew." Samantha shivered and wrapped her arms protectively across her chest. "We'll call Jordan when we get back to Dallas."

"I hope you don't mind, but I called Jordan while I was out to get him up to speed. So much has happened, and I figured he needed to start investigating Green Earth. Even if they didn't kill Joanna, the whole operation is shady as hell."

Before she could protest, Jack stopped pacing and pulled her out of the chair into his warm embrace. "Enough espionage. Now, I have a surprise for you. Put on something festive but warm."

"I know—a flannel cocktail dress. I think I have one here somewhere," she teased. "Come on, Jack." She nibbled his ear. "Where are we going?"

"No, you siren! You won't get me to tell!" He pushed her gently away, laughing. "You'll have to wait. It's a surprise. Now get dressed."

****

An hour later, he parked the car at a dock near Weirs Beach, close to a sign that read "Mount Washington." Moored at the end of a long dock was a small cruise ship.

"We're going on a boat?" Sam asked, her cat-green eyes as big as saucers.

"Not any old boat. We're going on a dinner cruise on Lake Winnipesaukee. I thought it might be a nice way to spend our last evening here."

She leaned over in the seat and kissed Jack until she was breathless.

"I take it you like the idea?" he asked, running the back of his hand across his ravaged lips, removing a telltale smear of lipstick.

"It's wonderful. I'm so glad you thought of it."

He helped her out of the car, and she looped her arm through his. Jack spread his hand protectively over hers.

As they walked up the gangplank to the railed deck, he couldn't keep his eyes off Sam. Her sleek body was poured into a skinny black dress, a stretchy, clingy affair. The dress covered every inch of her from neck to wrist to ankle but somehow revealed every curve to beautiful advantage.

Jack thought she must be a witch, all flashing green eyes and enchanting body, and if he didn't watch out, he would surely fall under her spell. Of course, there could be worse things, he mused as she walked onto the deck ahead of him, swaying provocatively in time to the lapping of the water on the shore.

Who was he kidding, anyway? It was already too late. Jack knew agreeing to follow Samantha to New Hampshire was a convenient excuse for spending time alone near her. He hadn't lied when he'd told her that. He hadn't realized it at first, but he had fallen for Samantha Morgan early on—maybe it was the day they went SCUBA diving or the night she told him about Gary; perhaps it was when he switched to a ceramic coffee mug. No matter, it had happened, and he was hooked on this little green-eyed siren as surely as he had told her he loved her.

That wasn't a lie either, and if things went as planned, he would fulfill his promise to Bobbie later that night. It might have started as a way to get on the plane to New Hampshire, but he knew now this was where he belonged—beside a woman who challenged him, stood up to him, and excited him more than any woman he had ever known.

If he could convince her he wasn't any of those other men who had hurt her, that he could offer her romance, security, and someone who would care for her in ways they never had, then maybe he could win her heart. Her body was already his; last night and this morning had proven that. But it was her trust he needed, her belief in him if he were to have a future with her.

It was her lack of trust that worried him. He had lied to her over and over. In fact, their entire relationship was founded on a lie about who he was and why he was at R.L. Morgan. Tonight, he would tell her the truth, beg her forgiveness, and end the lies for good. He prayed the love he knew they shared would be enough to counter her mistrust and accept what he wanted to give her.

And what he wanted to give her was a future together and all that entailed—a home filled with love and laughter and children—and two fat cats. A stable, secure life…complete and whole. And he would ask her to share it all with him. Later that evening, after a romantic moonlit cruise, when she had her fill of good food and excellent wine. After he had reaffirmed the covenant of love between them in the most physical of ways, he would confess his lies and ask for forgiveness and…her future in his arms.

"What are you thinking about? You're a million miles away." Samantha broke into his reverie as they crossed the dining room to the buffet table.

"Oh, nothing. I was thinking you look gorgeous tonight." He took her hand and kissed the palm, holding back the urge to kiss her sweet lips instead.

She squeezed his hand. "This is a wonderful surprise. Is this where you disappeared to this afternoon?"

"Yes," he answered, piling strips of succulent prime rib on his plate. "I had to drive to Weirs Beach to make the reservations. Mostly, I wanted to check out the boat. I didn't want you to be disappointed."

"Disappointed? It's fabulous! It's like a small cruise ship—right down to this incredible buffet. Mmm, these boiled shrimp look good." She found room on her plate for the shrimp and new potatoes swimming in butter and herbs.

Balancing salads and dinner plates, they wove their way back to a table in the corner, looking out onto the darkening lake. The dining room filled the entire upper level of the ship, ringed in plate glass windows framed in heavy maroon velvet curtains. Lighted candles flickered from gilt sconces on the walls between the windows. Strains of a concerto played by a string quartet drifted through the air.

It was an altogether different atmosphere than their dinner the previous night, being regaled by the raucous James Hoffman. Jack wondered briefly whether Hoffman had ever taken this cruise on the lake. Somehow, he doubted it.

Samantha relished every morsel of her dinner. Jack smiled, thinking her near-death experience hadn't slowed her appetite. She talked, gesturing animatedly, about Green Earth and what she had seen that day. Jack wasn't listening; he was mesmerized by her emerald eyes and the way her hair shimmered in the candlelight. He shook himself back to the moment.

Bewitched is a good word for it.

****

Jack eased the car into a narrow slot near the inn's front door. The wind had picked up considerably during the evening and gusted around the parking lot, whirling leaves at Samantha's feet. She shivered. It had gotten colder, too, and she was glad to have her long wool coat to snuggle into. It wasn't glamorous but certainly filled the bill, as winter seemed to knock on New Hampshire's door.

She and Jack hurried inside, gasping from the cold air. Brushing a leaf from the shoulder of her coat, Jack's hand stilled. Ten feet away, in a blue-checked wing chair, Detective Jordan sat, slightly amused as he peered over the top of his newspaper.

"Well, well, good evening," he said, smiling. "I

wondered when you two might be back."

"Jordan, what are you doing here?" Jack blurted.

Samantha wheeled around to face him. "Did you tell him to come?" Confusion welled up inside her like boiling water.

"No! I told him what was going on up here. That's all." He looked at her, his eyes cool gray, unreadable. Then, suddenly, they hardened to steel, and he turned on Jordan. "Why are you here?" he repeated.

Jordan lowered the paper and began folding it slowly, deliberately. "After the attempt on Miss Morgan's life this morning and the obvious illegal goings on at Green Earth…well, it seems you needed a little help in the bodyguard department. So, I came as soon as I could get a flight."

"What do you mean 'bodyguard department'?" Samantha demanded, still rooted to the spot by the door.

"You still haven't told her, Stone?"

"Told me what?" Samantha said through clenched teeth. "Jack, what's going on?"

"Look, Sam, I've been trying to find the right time to tell you. Let's go upstairs, and I'll explain everything." He grabbed her hand, but she jerked it away.

"No, tell me now. Here!"

"Good God, Stone! She deserves to know." Jordan stood up.

Slumping, Jack said, "Okay, Sam, at least sit and let me talk to you." He turned to Jordan. "And you, keep quiet."

Jordan raised his hands in surrender and sat down. Samantha reluctantly did the same.

"I work for a firm called Bolton's Valor Security and Investigations in Colorado. Your father hired me to come down to R.L. Morgan and work undercover to find out who sent threatening messages to Joanna."

Samantha shook her head, trying to process the lies. So many lies. "What threatening messages?"

"Joanna had been getting typed messages sent to the department warning her off *something.* No one knew what. I was brought in to find out who sent them. That's why I was talking to Joanna over lunch and dinner. She was the only one besides your father who knew who I am and why I have been at R.L. Morgan."

He pushed on. "After Joanna was murdered, my assignment expanded to include protecting you."

Jordan chuckled. "Shooting at the windmills and a car bomb. Great job, Stone."

Jack's rock-hard glare trained, laser-sharp, on Jordan. "That's enough. I think we're all aware I have not done my most stellar work here."

Memories of the recent weeks flooded in, crowding Samantha's thoughts. And Jack featured prominently in every one. Always there, insinuating himself into her days, her life. "Assignment? So that's what this is all about? An assignment? From my father?"

All of it was merely a job he had to do?

"We all knew you wouldn't accept police protection. And frankly, we didn't have enough hard evidence to warrant it. I was the logical choice to keep an eye on you."

The blood drained from her face, then instantly rushed in to fill the void. Her cheeks burned, and her eyes stung. "Keep an eye on me?" she choked, impaling Jack with her glare.

"Look, Sam, I…" Jack began.

"What about all the garbage about wanting to be

with me? You're only here because he—" She stabbed a finger in Jordan's direction. "—And my father sent you?"

"At first, yes, but…"

"Oh, God, Jack, the whole thing was a lie?" Tears spilled down her cheeks as she struggled for control. "All of it?"

Before he could answer or stop her, she jerked the car keys from his hand and flew out the door.

****

Jack yelled at her to stop, but his voice died on the wind.

He would have followed her, but Jordan gripped his arm. "Let her go for now. She needs to cool off. Miss Independent, isn't she?"

Jack debated whether to punch the stocky little man's face in or shove him to the ground. Instead, he turned away and collapsed into one of the wing chairs. "What the hell are you doing here? When I called you, we said we'd talk tomorrow. You've ruined everything."

"Sorry, Stone, I had no way of knowing you hadn't told Miss Morgan the truth yet. What do you mean 'ruined everything'?"

"We had rather important things to discuss tonight, and I didn't want her thinking about murder or convinced I'm a lying son of a bitch." He paused, a little embarrassed at having revealed even that little bit of personal information. "So, what are you doing here exactly? It's not because you think I need help."

Jordan put his fingertips together and studied them intently. "Right. We're convinced the Levinson murder has something to do with Green Earth."

"We've already established that."

"So, that's why I came. I want to see for myself what's going on at their plant. If what you've observed is true, we may need to get the Feds involved.

Jack whistled softly. "I'm getting her out of here tomorrow."

"Good idea. And, by the way, you're a target now, too. You two are joined at the hip. I'm pretty sure the car bomb and the attempt this morning were intended for both of you."

"Yeah, I know." Jack ran his hand through his hair. "We let her drive out of here! Knowing they want to kill her!"

"Look, Stone, no one's going after her in the middle of the night. They aren't expecting her to be out roaming around. They won't do anything 'til morning."

"I don't like this one bit."

"I'm afraid there's nothing we can do until she returns. Why don't you go up to your room? I'll wait here for her."

"No, I can't sleep. I'll see if I can find us some coffee."

He walked to the registration desk and, after considerable discussion, was directed to the coffee maker and supplies in the office directly behind it. Jack brewed a pot and watched the hot liquid stream slowly into the glass carafe.

He shook his head. What a mess. Now Sam thought the worst of him. Not that he didn't deserve it. He *had* lied to her. But somewhere along the line, the lie had become the truth. And now he didn't want her to think the truth was a lie. Too late. The way she had stormed out of the inn, there was no mistaking what she thought.

"I should have gone after her, stopped her," he

chastised himself. Why didn't she come back? She'd had plenty of time to calm down, get tired and cold. Or lost! Or what if she had car trouble? A flat tire? Hit a deer? He laughed at his own imagination. Then, sobering, Jack realized all he wanted was for her to walk through the door. He wanted to take her in his arms and make her believe the truth—that he loved her and wanted to marry her.

****

It was a full ten minutes after she fled the inn before Samantha admitted she had behaved foolishly. "What an idiot!" she muttered under her breath, her eyes straining to see through the dense fog that had settled on the woods around her like a shroud. "I took off running like I always do. Escaping the lies. Escaping the shame."

What did I expect? They all lie to me eventually.

She gave up trying to see through the solid gray mess and pulled the big car onto the narrow shoulder. Her flight from the inn had taken her out of the village and onto the road she and Jack had traversed daily on their way to Green Earth. She guessed she was a couple of miles from town now. Might as well stay put for a while and wait until the soup cleared.

Jack obviously wasn't concerned about her, she thought dejectedly, huddling deeper into her coat. He hadn't even tried to stop her. He could have taken Jordan's car and followed her. No, he'd probably gone to bed—tired of her silly school-girl tantrum.

And Jordan! Why had he come anyway? It couldn't be just because the car tried to run them down. It must be something more.

And Jack had been acting secretive all day. It was obvious he had planned something special for their evening, and Jordan's arrival certainly spoiled it. He was probably trying to ply her with wine and delicious food right before he told her the truth about who he was and what he was really up to. If he planned to tell her at all. More lies.

And her father! Why was he sticking his nose into this? She would give him a piece of her mind when she got home. He needed to quit meddling in her business. She was fully grown and could take care of herself. She didn't need all these men looking out for her! And it was about time she told them so!

She turned the key in the ignition. The car sputtered ominously, then sprang to life. Samantha breathed a sigh of relief. She turned on the headlights, illuminating the fog and little else. Carefully, she eased the car onto the road as a large truck careened past, heading back toward town. She barely missed hitting it. But she saw the word FISH stenciled on the side.

A split second later, she followed the truck as it crept down the narrow, wooded road. She snapped the headlights off and stayed far enough behind to avoid detection. It was tricky, but she kept the truck's taillights in sight despite the gray mist obscuring her vision.

After about a mile, the truck turned onto a secluded little trail. In all the times Samantha and Jack had been on the road, she had never even noticed the tiny trail. No signs or gates marked its entry, and branches from sturdy maple and birch trees camouflaged the opening. Samantha turned in behind the truck, which had slowed considerably to maneuver onto the narrow path.

The trail wound through the forest for about two miles. Samantha lost her sense of direction but knew the truck was moving farther away from town, deeper into the primeval forest that graced this part of the country. It crossed her mind this was the most enchanting place she'd ever been, even in the fog. And she was doing the dumbest thing she'd ever done.

At last, the truck slowed to a crawl as the trail closed in even further. It was as if the vehicle had been swallowed up by the forest. Samantha crept along until the path suddenly gave way to a wide clearing. About a hundred yards away was a cluster of one-story shacks, about six in all, each the size of a small cottage. A high chain-link fence, topped by three rows of spiky barbed wire surrounded the buildings. A single guard tower rose from the middle of the compound. A blinding spotlight on each corner illuminated the scene.

Samantha pulled the car off the trail and under a tree, quickly turning off the engine. Two burly men she recognized from earlier in the day climbed out of the truck and opened the back. It was empty! She had expected the truck to be making a delivery!

Fascinated, she stared as about a dozen men swarmed out of one of the buildings, wheeling racks of plastic-covered clothes like she and Jack had seen at Green Earth. Each man wore what looked like loose-fitting pajamas, and they were much smaller in stature than the truck drivers. They loaded the racks of clothes into the truck while the drivers stood by, their arms folded across their chests.

"I've got to tell Jack and Jordan." She pulled her cell phone out of her purse. No signal. They'd have to find out when she returned.

Her curiosity got the better of her and she left the car and skulked around the edge of the clearing in the shadows until she could get a closer peek. One of the shacks sat within a few feet of the fence line, its single window facing her. She ran to the fence. Standing on tiptoe, she could barely see through the grimy glass.

Inside were about a dozen Asian people, including children, dressed in the same pajama-styled clothing as the men outside. They sat at sewing machines, working fabric forward and back, piecing together the garments Samantha had seen in the showroom at Green Earth. They labored shoulder to shoulder under bare-bulb lighting. A virtual mountain of partially finished garments filled the corner.

From her vantage point, she could see the other shacks had similar windows and lights on inside, although she couldn't see people in them from where she stood.

She clicked a few pictures of the inside of the shack and the surrounding buildings, the fence, and the guard tower, then shoved her phone in her coat pocket.

"Slave labor!" A sickening knot tightened in her stomach. "Joanna must have known!" Then, as the panic rose like bile in her throat, she hurried back to the safety of the car.

She turned the key in the ignition. Nothing. No grinding. No sputtering. No clicking. Just a thunderous silence. The panic in her throat burned hot and tasted bitter. She had to get out of there and back to town. She had to tell Detective Jordan why Joanna was killed. She had to tell Jack why Green Earth could make so many garments using so few employees. She had to help these people escape this horrible place.

She got out of the car, thinking she would walk toward town and get a cell signal, and stepped into the broad chest of the same man who had told them to leave

Green Earth that morning. A work-roughened hand grabbed her arm and jerked her to within inches of his unshaven face. He smelled faintly of beer.

He growled. "Thought I told you to leave."

She wished she could do that when a blow of such force hit the back of her head it caused her to fall forward into the flannel-clad arms of the truck driver.

Then everything went black.

****

Jack contained himself a full hour, calling her cell every five minutes and getting no answer before he commandeered Jordan's rented car to look for Sam. He folded his lengthy frame into the compact car, muttering something about the cheapness of the Key West police force. Then he sped out of the inn parking lot and down the hill toward the lake. He intersected the main road out of town, pausing only a moment before turning toward Green Earth. He hoped in the heat of anger she would take a familiar route.

The heavy fog from the lake blanketed the road, slowing his progress.

"Dammit!" Jack pounded the steering wheel with his fist. "I'll never find her at this rate. Hell, if I went right past her, I wouldn't even know it."

He crawled down the narrow silver ribbon, hoping to see a sign of their rental car. Thirty minutes later, on a whim, he pulled into the parking lot of Green Earth. The huge halogen lights broke through the gray mist enough to wash the area in a surreal glow.

"They're sure not working through the night to make their production quota," he mused absently.

A thorough study of the near-empty lot revealed one medium-sized sedan, parked near the front door, an old station wagon, its windows broken out, abandoned in the shadows at the edge of the tree line, and a couple of the trucks marked FISH he and Samantha had seen earlier in the day.

"She's not here," Jack said aloud. "Not that I thought she would be. What would she be doing here, anyway?"

He arced the car around the lot and steered again onto the road.

"She's probably back at the inn by now, and I'm wandering around for nothing," he muttered, trying to convince himself. He called Jordan, only to hear she had yet to return. He called Sam again. Still no answer.

Jack was worried. A knot formed in his stomach that tightened as the minutes ticked by. He began to sweat. Exasperated at Sam's uncanny ability to worry him, he swore softly, shrugged out of his overcoat, and drove back to the inn.

Minutes later, the knot in his stomach turned to stone when the rental was not in the hotel parking lot. Jack stormed into the lobby to find Detective Jordan still sitting where he had left him an hour earlier. Jordan looked over the top of the newspaper when Jack slammed the door behind him. He noticed it was the same section of the paper Jordan had been reading all night. *So, he's worried, too.*

"She's not back. She's not answering her phone. It's been two hours. I think she's had plenty of time to cool off, don't you?" Jack asked, collapsing into a chair.

Jordan folded the paper again and set it aside. "Yes, she should have returned by now."

"What do you think we should do? Call the police?" Then he added sarcastically, "No, wait, it seems to me the police are already here, and a fat lot of good they're doing!"

Ignoring his sarcasm, Jordan spoke calmly, "I've already alerted the Meredith police. I called them after you left."

"Well, what are they doing?"

"She must be missing twenty-four hours before they'll do anything formally."

"And informally?"

"They're looking for her."

"Where?"

"Mostly patrolling the roads leading out of Meredith."

"Well, she's not anywhere on the one we've been on this week—the one that goes back and forth to Green Earth."

Jordan sat up straighter. "You drove to Green Earth?"

"Yeah, but she wasn't there."

The detective stood. "I'm going to my room. You did book a room for me, didn't you, Stone?"

Jack glared at him. "I didn't know you were coming, remember? They don't have any vacant rooms, but you can have the one they've been holding for me."

"Holding for you? Where have you been staying?"

"Never mind, I'll tell you in the morning. Now that Sam is furious with me, you and I may be roommates," he said, and a deep feeling of loss gripped him. He had to find her. "I think I'll go back out and look. I can't sleep."

"All right, check in every hour or so," Jordan said. "I won't be sleeping either."

Chapter Twelve

Samantha lay on the beach, the waves washed over her naked body in a warm rhythm, caressing her, teasing her, and enveloping her. Overhead, the sun shone brightly, playing hide-and-seek amidst the fluffy clouds. Jack leaned over, smiling, bending closer for a kiss. Then, a dark cloud moved in front of him, blocking Samantha's view, turning noon to dusk in an instant, casting a shadow over her. She shivered as the warming rays cooled and the water chilled her to the bone.

The dark cloud scooped her up from the sand and carried her to the rocks. Her head hurt where a stone pillowed it. She struggled to move, to run back to Jack, to the soothing water, but the cloud prevailed, covering her face until the world went black.

****

At six a.m., when Jack returned to the inn for the third time, Jordan punched off his cell phone and informed him the Meredith police had found the rental car abandoned near Weir's Beach. The keys were in the ignition. Samantha's purse was inside. But there was no other sign of her.

"Weir's Beach? Why would she go there?" Jack paced the floor in Jordan's room. "Where's the car now?"

"They had it towed."

"I thought you said the keys were in the ignition."

"They were, but the car wouldn't start—the battery's dead. They towed it to a station here in town."

Jack stopped directly in front of Jordan, his ever-present notepad on the table beside him. "The car wouldn't start? Maybe Sam went for help. Have they checked the woods around the car? The road? Maybe she went into Weir's Beach to phone since you can't get a signal in the woods. Where's her cell?"

"The police in Weir's Beach are checking now. They haven't found her cell. It seems Samantha vanished."

Jack grabbed his overcoat from the chair he had slung it across. As he turned to the door, he saw himself in the mirror and barely recognized the ashen face reflected there, mouth as hard as iron, steel-cold eyes shadowed by dark, sleep-deprived circles, jaw muscles twitching imperceptibly. He still wore his navy suit from the evening before, tie askew and jacket wrinkled.

He turned his back on the madman in the mirror and said deliberately, "She hasn't vanished. Hoffman has her. And I'm going to get her. If you want to come, I'll meet you in the lobby in fifteen minutes."

Seconds later, he opened the door to the room he and Samantha had shared for the past three days. It was as he and Sam had left it the night before, suitcases open, towels hanging in the bath, toiletries on the counter, clothes in the closet. Jack's breath caught in his throat when he saw the sheet still dangling from its single clothespin. Was it only two nights ago he had torn down the barrier between them?

He grabbed the remaining sheet and ripped it from the line. "I won't lose her now!" he growled and tore it apart, letting the jagged pieces flutter to the floor.

****

Samantha struggled to stay above the swelling sea. She'd been swimming toward the shore for hours, but every stroke in the undulating current carried her farther out. The warm water blanketed her. It would be easy to stop swimming and let it cover her, cocooned in liquid comfort. Then she saw Jack on the shore, beckoning her, urging her in. She'd keep swimming for Jack, only Jack.

Her arms and legs were stronger; she made headway. Then Jack disappeared. The shoreline, empty now, seemed to recede and grow dim. It was better to stay in the water, safe in the water, wrapped in the water. Grateful, Samantha let the darkness engulf her once more.

****

Jordan had convinced Jack they should check out the car before they barreled into Hoffman's office. So, he stopped the car first at the service station where several Meredith police officers and the auto mechanic were standing around discussing Samantha's disappearance. When they inspected the car, they found nothing new, but Jack had a hunch.

"I think they towed the car."

"Yeah, I told you. It was towed from the beach to here," Jordan reminded him.

"No, I mean towed *to* Weir's Beach."

"You mean Samantha didn't drive to Weir's Beach?"

"Right. I think she would have gone in a familiar direction."

"Toward Green Earth?"

"Exactly. Then she stopped. Maybe the fog forced her off the road. Maybe she went to the plant. God knows. When she was ready to turn the car back on, the battery was dead. She couldn't get a cell signal, so she got out to get help, and someone from Green Earth grabbed her."

"Sounds plausible. They would have towed the car someplace in the opposite direction."

"Right, to send us on a wild goose chase."

Jordan sighed and wrote a few notes on his pad. "It seems our Miss Morgan may have speeded up everyone's plans."

Jack swallowed the fear that threatened to choke him. He had to focus on getting her back and trying to stay calm. For Sam's sake. "Okay, send a SWAT Team or something, and we'll go after her."

The Meredith police lieutenant cleared his throat. "It's not quite that easy, Mr. Stone. Meredith is a small place. We don't have a SWAT Team. But we have competent officers who will check out this idea you and Detective Jordan have. I must say, however, I've known James Hoffman for several years. He's a model citizen and community supporter. I can't imagine him being mixed up in this sort of thing—kidnapping, murder. Impossible."

For a split second, Jack considered wringing the officer's scrawny little neck. Fortunately, Jordan intervened in a voice that could have melted rocks, "Lt. Henderson, Mr. Stone and I have been working on this case for a while. I assure you we would not attempt to smudge anyone's good reputation without cause. And you can take this to the bank: we have cause.

"Furthermore, if you send officers to the plant and inquire about Miss Morgan, that will tip our hand, and we will lose her for sure." He leaned in close to

Henderson and narrowed his shrewd, brown eyes. "These people have killed one woman already, Lieutenant. I wouldn't want *you* to be responsible for another murder."

The youthful officer swallowed and shifted nervously from one foot to the other. "What do you suggest, then, Detective?"

"I think Mr. Stone and I should pay a little call on James Hoffman—strictly business, of course. They don't need to know who I am. I'll be a colleague of Stone's."

Regaining his composure enough to protest, the Lieutenant insisted a squad car follow along in case of trouble. Jordan agreed reluctantly, whispering to Jack, "I guess I shouldn't push my luck. I'm out of my jurisdiction here, all the way around."

****

The beautiful coral reef waved gently in the crystal-clear water. Samantha wanted to reach out, to become one in its rhythmic movement, but she knew her touch would be deadly. She could see Joanna amid the reef, swaying as if hypnotized by the motion—back and forth, back and forth—Samantha swam closer.

Joanna disappeared into the reef. Laughter bubbled up from inside the coral, and Samantha followed, swimming deep into the formation. But the rosy fingers gripped her ankles, dragging her down into the depths of the reef until the laughter echoed in the closing darkness.

****

Jack and Jordan watched the front door of the Green Earth plant from inside the detective's rental car. The Meredith police had impounded Jack's Lincoln pending further investigation, so he was forced to go in Jordan's compact, his knees uncomfortably bumping the dashboard. It was bad enough he had driven in that torturous position all night, but now his patience was wearing thin.

"I know she's here. God knows what they've done to her by now." He opened the passenger door. "I'm going in."

"Stone! Wait!" Jordan tried to grab him, but it was too late. He got out and followed Jack to the entrance.

Jack strode to the doorway, glad to be out of the confines of the car but mostly relieved to be *doing* something to get Samantha back. He pushed the double doors open and nodded to the receptionist as he went directly up the stairs to Hoffman's office.

Alarmed, she stood and called out to Jack. When he didn't stop, she reached for the phone to call Security. Jordan, puffing along behind, flashed his badge at the woman so she could see it was official but little else. She promptly sat down, still holding the receiver.

"Strictly business, huh, Stone? Damn," Jordan muttered irritably. "He'll alert the whole place."

Hoffman's secretary received roughly the same greeting as the receptionist, as Jack and Jordan burst through the heavy wooden doors unannounced.

"Hoffman, we're here to…" Jack stopped in his tracks. The room was empty. No Hoffman. No Samantha.

The secretary bustled in behind them. "I'm sorry, sir, Mr. Hoffman left on a business trip earlier this morning."

Jordan whipped out his notepad. "May I see his itinerary?"

"Well, I'm not authorized to divulge that information."

"Miss—er—" He checked the nameplate on her desk. "Buckraven, I'm sure you want to cooperate with the police. They're right outside. I'll call them." He moved to the door.

The frightened woman sank into her chair. "I'll tell you what you want to know. Let's not cause a scene. I'll lose my job if there's a scene. Please don't tell Mr. Hoffman I told you." She pulled up a screen on the computer, printed a copy of the itinerary, and handed it to Jordan.

"Tell me one other thing, Miss Buckraven," Jordan asked, studying the paper. "Was there a woman with Mr. Hoffman when he left?"

"A woman?"

"Miss Morgan," Jack said. "The woman who has been here this week."

The secretary shook her head. "There was no woman at all. I certainly would have recognized Miss Morgan." She added wistfully, "She is so beautiful."

Jack winced.

After a brief conversation with Lt. Henderson, he and Jordan returned to the car and began a procession to the private airport the secretary said Hoffman used. Jack studied the itinerary while Jordan drove.

It indicated Hoffman was flying to North Carolina at ten a.m., probably to the fabric manufacturing plant. Despite what Miss Buckraven said, he knew Samantha would be on that plane. She had to be. The alternative was too horrible to consider. He prayed he would get to the airport in time.

He didn't.

When they pulled up to the little prefabricated building that served as an office, the wizened old man behind a battered desk told them the plane had taken off.

"They were in a powerful hurry. Loaded a big crate onto the plane and took off. I had to practically chase 'em down to get the fight plan."

"You got a flight plan?"

"Yes, sir, here it is."

Jordan snatched the paper from the gnarled hand. "Beacham Field near Raleigh."

Jack turned to the old man. "Is there another plane here? One we could rent?"

"Well, yeah, old Joe has one over there." He gestured toward an aging twin engine in a field of high grass. "But he ain't here right now."

"Does it fly?"

"Yup, it flies."

"Gas it up. I'll take it."

"But I told you, old Joe ain't here."

Jordan stared at him, dumbfounded. "What are you thinking, Stone?"

"I'm thinking I'm going to North Carolina in old Joe's transport."

"You've got to be kidding. Can you fly?"

"Yeah, I flew in the service."

"But you were in the Navy."

Jack raised one eyebrow in question. "Right, the Navy has the best pilots around," he snapped. "Your investigation of my background wasn't comprehensive enough."

"Sorry, just routine. Do you think you can fly that plane?"

"If it's got wings, I can fly it," Jack said, voicing a bravado he didn't necessarily feel. But he knew catching a commercial flight to Raleigh would take hours. Then, even longer to get to Beacham. This was the fastest way to stop Hoffman. He hoped he could get there in time.

****

Samantha heard voices, but she couldn't see the faces they belonged to. She swam up through a sea of unconsciousness to a blurred light, struggling for control. At last, she burst through the surface of awareness and opened her eyes.

Her head ached and moving it hurt. But she could take in a limited view of her surroundings. She lay on the seat of a car. Several men sat across from her. A limousine!

"She's awake," one of the men said.

"The boss said to leave her alone if she woke up again," the one beside him said.

The men seemed vaguely familiar, but in her muddled state, Samantha couldn't place them. She tried to sit up, but a stabbing pain shot from the back of her head down to her shoulder.

Gingerly, she lifted one hand to her head and fingered the gash, about an inch long, slicing through a swollen, tender area the size of an egg. The hair around the cut was matted and sticky. When she pulled her fingers away, they were bloodstained.

"Ole Billy Boy got you pretty good, didn't he?" The first man laughed.

Samantha took her hand away, lay back on the seat, and closed her eyes again.

It crossed her mind Billy Boy had tried to kill her, and she might die even now, but the sickly grogginess overwhelmed her before the fear did, and she drifted back into a dreamless sleep.

****

Jack lowered the nose of the plane and leveled off. He eased the power and the props back until the gauges read 25/25. Then he leaned the engines for his cruising altitude.

Jordan sunk against the window on the passenger side, his face a queasy shade of green.

"What's the matter, Jordan? Airsick? Do you always get sick when you fly?"

"No, I usually take something and sleep on flights. But we left so fast. I hardly had time to stop at the drug store now, did I?" He groaned softly and leaned his head back against the window. "Can't you hold this thing still?"

"It's the heat rising through the atmosphere. Causes turbulence on take-offs and landings."

By mid-afternoon, the plane reached Beacham Field, and Jack began his approach to the little airfield near Raleigh. He knew he was rusty in the cockpit and hadn't landed a plane in years. But the training he received in the Navy came back like a familiar routine.

Drop the gear and flaps to slow the plane. Chop the throttle. No, the runway's too short. I'm gonna be hot and long.

The plane touched down, going too fast. Jack stood on the brakes to keep from careening off the end of the runway. The plane skidded to a stop next to a barbed wire fence.

He taxied to the little shack where the fixed base operator would be. The plane wobbled as it went, and not only because holes and rough patches pocked the asphalt runway. The tires were flat in one spot where the rubber had worn away when the plane landed. "Can't wait until Old Joe sees this," he muttered.

Jordan got out of the plane and promptly threw up.

Jack rushed into the building and practically accosted the tiny, middle-aged woman behind the desk. "Did a corporate plane from New Hampshire land here today?"

"Yes, sir, one did."

"Where are they? Did they go into Raleigh? Was there a woman with them?"

"No, sir, I didn't see a woman. They didn't stay, but refueled and left."

"They're not here? Where did they go?"

The woman squared her shoulders and looked unflinchingly at Jack. "I don't think I should give out that kind of information, sir."

Jordan came in and flashed his badge as he had in Hoffman's office, without the same effect.

"May I see that a little closer, please," the woman asked calmly.

Jordan shrugged and handed the wallet over. The woman clucked her tongue, shook her head, then handed it back.

"I'm afraid you have no power here, Detective Jordan. And shame on you for trying to take advantage of me."

Jack stepped in front of the detective, who looked a little sheepish.

"Ma'am," Jack said in his most charming tone. "You're absolutely right. We have no power here, but I'm desperate to find out what happened to that plane. You see, they've kidnapped the woman I love, and they may be about to murder her if we don't get there first. That's why the detective is here. Please, you have to help me."

Jordan's head shot up at the word "love," and he stared in silent awe as the woman rushed to get the flight plan and give it to Jack.

He and Jordan spoke together, "Key West!"

Jack ran his hand through his disheveled hair. "Dear God, he's going to kill her in the same place he murdered Joanna. We've got to get going."

"I'm not going with you. I can't get in that thing again. I'll go to Raleigh and get a flight from there. I'll be in Key West late tonight, but not much after you, I imagine. In the meantime, I'll contact my people and get them to look out for Hoffman's plane. Ten-to-one, this whole thing will be taken care of by the time you get there."

Jack was not so sure. "I hope so." Then, he turned to the woman, who wrung her hands at the mention of Joanna's murder. "Will you see the plane gets gassed up? Can I get coffee anywhere?"

"Yes, hon, there's coffee over there. Help yourself. And I'll get you out of here in two shakes. Lordy, I hope that girl of yours is all right. Murder, Lord, Lord, what is this world coming to?" She muttered to herself as she picked up the intercom and barked orders at someone Jack hoped was a mechanic on duty. For a fleeting moment, he smiled, thinking how the feisty lady held her ground with Jordan.

Twenty minutes later, he took off from Beacham Field, leaving Jordan on his cell, looking immensely relieved. Jack checked his watch. He would have to fly until about eight o'clock, then land at the county airport in Key West.

His eyelids were heavy after two hours in the air, and the instrument panel seemed to play tricks on him, numbers dancing in the lights. Once or twice, he dozed off but jerked awake when the plane hit an air pocket. The fear of drifting off course was enough to keep him awake until he heard the voice of the control tower in Key West telling him he was clear to land.

****

Samantha's head pounded, but she considered that a good sign. At least she wasn't dead, no thanks to Billy Boy. She had awakened about an hour earlier when they carried her from the limousine into a warehouse building and unceremoniously dumped her on a worn-out vinyl couch in a grimy office.

The same flannel-clad bully who caught her at the labor compound had done the carrying and the dumping, and now, it seemed, he did the guarding. The burly man sat across from her in a metal folding chair, arms crossed over his chest as they had been at the compound. He eyed her beneath hooded lids.

But this wasn't Billy Boy, the faceless one who had come up behind her and knocked her half crazy. Where was he? Never mind. It was too painful to think.

All she wanted was for the headache to go away and Jack to save her. It must have been hours since she was caught at the compound. She had no way of knowing how long she had been unconscious. But by now, Jack and Jordan would be looking for her. They'd figure out Hoffman had her and come get her.

They might already be here, wherever "here" was. Maybe Hoffman's goons had taken her to another building Green Earth owned near Meredith. She was sure Jack would figure out where she was. It wouldn't be long before he broke down the door and rescued her.

Maybe if she closed her eyes, the headache would

ease up a little.

****

"So, Miss Morgan, I hear you're back among us. I'm sorry Bill thought it necessary to hit you so hard. I would have preferred a gentler approach."

Samantha recognized the soothing sounds of the man who had come into the office. She opened her eyes to see Elgin Lenhart crouching beside her, his face very close to hers.

"Ah, there you are. Let me help you up. Would you like something to drink?"

"Water, please," Samantha croaked, her mouth as dry as toast.

"Certainly." He walked to a desk where a carafe of water and a couple of glasses had been placed and poured a drink.

He handed it to Samantha, who sipped it gratefully. Her head still swam, and she felt woozy and weak.

"Where are we?" she asked when she finished the water.

"Oh, someplace safe. You don't need to know where. We'll stay here until Mr. Hoffman finalizes his plans."

"What plans?" she asked, her voice barely above a whisper.

He smiled politely. "Plans for you, of course."

She thought she might faint but steadied her hand against the arm of the couch. "Me? What do you mean, plans for me?" As the grogginess lifted, a new and frightening awareness gripped Samantha. Elgin Lenhart was not here to help her.

She had to do something. If she took the offensive, she might talk her way out. "Mr. Lenhart, you know you can't get away with this. Jack Stone and Detective Jordan from the Key West police knew where I was going. I'm sure they're following me even now. They probably saw your little slave labor operation, too. Kidnapping me will do you no good. You'd have to take me halfway across the country to hide me from those two men."

"Exactly, Miss Morgan. Exactly," Lenhart said quietly, then left the room, locking the door behind him.

****

The scraping of a key in the lock awakened Samantha sometime later. Shadows played in the corners of the room. It must be dark out, she thought. An overhead light snapped on, and James Hoffman filled the room. She lifted her head from the vinyl. Her neck was stiff and sore, and her head still throbbed.

"Miss Morgan, I guess we won't be doing business after all," he said, his voice syrupy sweet.

Samantha winced. "Let me go, Hoffman, while you still have a chance." Her voice held as much conviction as she could muster.

"So, you can run to that sap, Stone, and tell him what you saw?"

"You're running a slave labor camp, aren't you?"

The big man smiled and nodded. "I suppose you could say that. I prefer to think of it as helping to ease our immigration problems."

From behind him, the flannel-clad bully laughed. Elgin Lenhart, who now joined Hoffman, stood quietly to one side. His expression didn't change.

"You're holding those people prisoner. Why didn't you give them jobs in the plant?"

"It was a business decision, Miss Morgan. When I took over Green Earth, it was severely in debt. We needed to cut back on payroll but keep production and quality high. On my travels to Asia, we arranged transport for a boatload of people who wanted to escape North Korea. They were glad to pay me to bring them to the good old U.S. of A. When they arrived in Boston, we smuggled them into Meredith and settled them in their new home.

"We taught them to make the garments. They're good workers, especially with a little nudging from Bill occasionally. And we pay them a small wage each month. Of course, they must buy everything they need from our company store there at the camp. They're simple people, Miss Morgan. We got them out of North Korea. We pay them for their work. They have food and clothes and a place to live. They think they're living the American dream!"

Flannel Guy hooted out loud. Nausea swept over Samantha.

"The American Dream?" she screeched, ignoring the pain in her head. "You've done nothing but exploit their predicament to line your own pockets. Simple people! They're not simple people! They have intelligence and dignity. They came here to be free from an oppressive government, and instead, they're oppressed by you!" She took a breath, then plunged on, "You're despicable, you…you…slave trader!"

The exertion drained her of any energy she had built up, and she slumped back against the couch.

Lenhart looked amused by her tirade. "Very noble, Miss Morgan," he said. "But I'm afraid your bleeding-heart notions won't work here."

Samantha was unutterably weary. "What are you going to do with me? Kill me like you did Joanna?"

Hoffman, who had been chuckling, quit smiling and closed the gap between the door and the couch in one stride. He jerked Samantha to a standing position. Her legs wobbled. She would have fallen to the floor, but he held her up by her shoulders. His fingers dug into her flesh.

"What do you know about that?" he growled, his face inches from hers.

"I know you killed her, you bastard. You were dating, and somehow, she found out about your slave camp. So, you met her during our convention in Key West, and you killed her while you were snorkeling."

Hoffman abruptly let her go, shoving her slightly back onto the couch. He laughed out loud and turned to Lenhart. "Tell her what happened."

The birdlike man sat on the couch next to Samantha. "Miss Morgan, I'm afraid you've been laboring under a misapprehension of the truth."

"Excuse me?"

"It wasn't Mr. Hoffman who was dating Joanna. It was I. We knew each other from high school. We ran into each other after all those years when she visited Green Earth. She was quite beautiful, and I dearly loved her, but when she discovered our little compound, she threatened to go to the authorities. I couldn't let her do that; after all, I was the one who had made most of the arrangements regarding the transportation and encampment of the North Koreans.

"So, I assured her I would see to it the people were set free and compensated for the time they had worked. She seemed satisfied enough. I think she loved me, too." He paused briefly, looking a little wistful, then continued, "We arranged to go snorkeling while she was in Key West. I told her I was going to be on the island for business. We have several other businesses operating out of the Keys, you see. So, Bill drove us to the reef in the company boat. She looked beautiful in the very alluring tiger-striped swimsuit. And while we were snorkeling, Bill swam down to us and strangled her. I couldn't have done it, you understand."

He clasped his hands in his lap and stared down at them.

Panic built within Samantha, and she knew she would probably not see Jack or her parents again unless she stalled for time. Time for Jack and Jordan to find her.

These were crazy people. Lenhart had murdered the woman he loved, and Hoffman had no regard for human life. But they were arrogant. Maybe if she kept them talking about themselves…

"Well, you certainly fooled us. We had it completely wrong. Was it you who tried to run me down in Meredith?"

"Oh, it was that lug head, Bill." Hoffman shook his head. "We were following you to see how much you knew. When he saw you alone, he decided on his own to take you out. Stupid son-of-a-bitch. There in broad daylight on Main Street. I nearly killed *him* for doing something so—obvious."

"So, I guess you shot at me at Eco-Tek, too?"

"Eco-Tek? In Frisco? No, we didn't follow you until you got to Meredith." He seemed puzzled. "Someone shot at you at Eco-Tek?" He shook his head. "Well, it wasn't us. I wish it had been, though. Should have taken care of you a lot sooner."

Samantha's palms were sweating. "Sooner than what?"

"Sooner than now, Miss Morgan."

Chapter Thirteen

With her hands tied behind her back it was nearly impossible for Samantha to keep her balance in the delivery van as it careened through the twisting and turning streets. Flannel Guy crouched in the corner by the double doors at the back, his hands splayed against the walls to steady himself.

They had piled her into the vehicle inside the warehouse. She couldn't tell if it were day or night, and she had no idea where she was or where they were taking her. Chances were, neither did Jack. That realization filled her with despair.

The van hit a bump and lurched crazily, toppling her over on her side. Flannel Guy lost his balance, too, and clumsily righted himself. Samantha searched the empty van for something to hold onto or wedge herself against. She inched her way toward the front and found a metal ring bolted to the floor, used to tie down cargo.

Well, I'm cargo tonight.

She scooted back against the ring and held on. It only helped a little. Mostly, it made her arms ache.

The brakes squealed, and she was thrown forward. Her hands were jerked from the ring, and she hit her head on the wall. The van spun out of control, and Flannel Guy fell into the double doors. They opened under the force of the blow, and he flew out.

Samantha tumbled around in the back of the van,

every turn moving her closer to the gaping doors. When she reached the edge and was about to be thrown out, the van came to rest with a thud.

Shaken and bleeding from a cut on her forehead, she rolled out the open doors and into soft sand, struggling to her feet. She hid behind the van, getting her bearings. The vehicle leaned on three wheels against a metal guard rail. Behind them, a small car was parked on the road, hood up, but no driver was in sight. The van driver must have swerved to avoid hitting it and lost control. She peeked around the side of the van as he stumbled out of the cab, his face bloodied. But she didn't see Flannel Guy anywhere.

She had to move fast.

She spied a stand of tall marsh grass about fifty yards away and staggered toward it as quickly as she could. Her tied hands hindered her balance, and the soft sand beneath her feet slowed her progress. Hopefully, she would be safely away by the time the driver discovered her gone.

Peeking through the grass, she made out the driver in the van's headlights. He was dragging the body of Flannel Guy into the light.

Samantha turned around and wove her way through the grass to the other side. She stopped cold when she found herself on the beach, staring at the incoming tide.

The ocean! I'm at the ocean! Good God, where have they taken me?

She made her way back to the wall of grass and followed it around the edge of the beach until a welcoming light punctuated the darkness. A cheerful bungalow stood on stilts about a hundred yards from a dock where a pleasure boat was moored.

She stumbled toward it, willing herself to stay conscious. She reached the front of the house where a riot of flowers grew out of a dozen clay pots, and a hand-painted sign by the door declared the house belonged to The Brightons.

Samantha dragged herself up the steps to the deck and called out, being careful not to alert the driver to her whereabouts. "Help! Help! Somebody help me!" She knocked on the door, using what little strength she had left.

It swung open and an older man in a plaid bathrobe gaped at her.

Samantha collapsed in a heap on the deck.

The man stooped to help her up and called back over his shoulder, "Jeannie, call 911 and ask for an ambulance, then get out here."

A minute later, Jeannie appeared in the doorway wearing a fluffy chenille robe, running her hand through soft red curls. "Good Lord, Ed, what—?" She hurried to help Ed get Samantha into the house.

****

Jack had insisted on driving the police squad car Jordan commandeered in Key West. Zooming through narrow streets, Jack struggled to keep up with the car carrying Lenhart and another enormous man Jack had never seen. Jordan, in the passenger seat, grabbed the dashboard to steady himself.

Lenhart's car flew toward the beach, but where? Jack followed him, matching him turn for turn, but keeping a discreet distance.

A report of a wreck on a road out near the dunes came over the police radio; a van turned over, a body nearby.

God, please don't let it be Sam.

What the hell had happened in New Hampshire? Where was Hoffman? Did he have Sam? And where was Lenhart racing to? The wreck? Sam? It must be to Sam. It had to be to Sam.

Another call came over the radio. A young woman had collapsed at a house on the shore. They needed an ambulance. Jordan barked orders into the radio.

She's alive!

He couldn't lose sight of Lenhart, even though Jordan had scribbled down the address of the house that had placed the 911 call, even though the GPS squawked with directions every few minutes.

If Lenhart got there first, he would kill Sam and get away.

I can't let that happen.

Jack gripped the wheel and pressed his foot harder on the gas.

****

Samantha swayed precariously. Ed steadied her while Jeannie untied her hands. Sam clung to Ed as he steered her to a blue-striped sofa where she sat heavily, putting one hand to her forehead.

Jeannie moved Samantha's hand, discovering the cut underneath. "Ed, go get me a bowl of warm water and a couple of towels."

Ed did as he was told.

"What's your name, hon?" Jeannie asked, carefully inspecting the cut.

"Samantha…Samantha Morgan," Samantha stammered. Then she grabbed Jeannie's arm and pleaded. "Help me, please; there are men trying to kill me."

"Someone's done something to you all right," the older woman said as she found the lump and caked-over gash on the back of Samantha's head. "Help's on the way. Don't you worry."

"Call Jack, please," Samantha wailed, her last ounce of control gone. "I need Jack."

"Who's Jack? Tell me how…"

Two men burst through the back door.

Samantha screamed and grasped Jeannie like a terrified child.

"Miss Morgan, you shouldn't have left without a word. You've had us all so worried," Elgin Lenhart said, his voice clipped and oozing sarcasm. "I'm afraid you'll have to come back with me."

Ed entered the room from the kitchen, holding a bowl of water and a towel. He stopped mid-stride. "I think we'll let her wait here for the ambulance we called. She's obviously hurt. I don't think she should move."

Lenhart narrowed his eyes, his mouth a tight line. "I don't think you understand. Miss Morgan is in our care. She must come with us."

He motioned toward the huge man standing slightly behind him, wearing a T-shirt and cut-off shorts that exposed bulging, oversized muscles. His thick brows defined a protruding forehead shading his expressionless eyes. Samantha's fleeting thought was he was more ape than man. "Bill, will you gather Miss Morgan so we can take her home?"

Bill lifted Samantha from the sofa in spite of the vigorous protests of the Brightons. She screamed again and beat his brick-wall chest to no avail. He held her as if she were a squirming newborn.

The front door crashed open.

"Put her down."

Samantha turned to see Jack standing there, his eyes like silver daggers. Next to him Detective Jordan, equally menacing, had his revolver steadily trained on Bill.

"Jack!" Samantha screamed and struggled against her captor.

"Put her down," Jack repeated in even tones edged with steel.

Lenhart inched his way over to stand in front of Bill. "Come, Bill, they won't take a chance on hurting Miss Morgan. I believe we can leave now quite safely." They slowly backed toward the door.

Jordan shifted the gun slightly, so the barrel pointed at Lenhart's nose. "Stop right there. I can take you out without getting anywhere near Samantha. You should call it a day and let these folks get back to sleep."

Lenhart laughed, but there was no humor in his voice. "You must be joking. Why would I give in to you when I have the upper hand? I have the girl."

Jack rushed across the room and struck Lenhart with a right to the jaw. The little man staggered backward to the couch. Jack turned toward Bill. With a grunt, he tossed Samantha into the air like a sack of potatoes and fled out the back door.

****

Jack caught Sam before she hit the floor, scooping her into his arms, then moved to the side of the room, shielding her from any action to come.

She clutched at his neck and buried her head in his shoulder, sobbing.

He whispered to her, "It's all right, now, Sweetheart, I have you. It's all over." He took in the bruises on her arms, the gash on her forehead, and the blood matted in her hair. He kissed her gently on her smudged cheek.

What have they done to you?

Four uniformed police officers came charging in, guns drawn.

One of them said to Jordan. "We have them, sir, you can stand down."

His hand shaking, Jordan holstered his gun and growled at Lenhart, "It seems I now have the upper hand." Then he said to the officer, "Arrest him. The other one, too. He went out the back."

"On what grounds, sir?"

"Kidnapping and assault for starters. We'll see what else we can drum up."

Certain the danger was over, Jack carried Sam out the front door and to the waiting ambulance.

Half a dozen officers came around the back of the house leading Bill in handcuffs.

Samantha cringed at the sight of him and said between rasping gasps for air, "Jack, they were going to k-k-kill me."

It was only when the paramedics put her on the gurney that Jack let her go. But he insisted on driving in the ambulance beside her, holding her hand on the ride to the hospital.

As he watched her drift off into a drugged sleep, he thought about what he might have done to Lenhart and that gorilla Bill if Jordan hadn't been there. He had never known such rage.

But mostly it was his own guilt that tore at him. He squeezed Samantha's hand, birdlike in his.

I failed her again.

****

After the squad cars containing Lenhart and Bill drove way, Jordan introduced himself to the Brightons.

A few minutes later, Jeannie poured him a cup of coffee, then she and Ed sat across from him at the kitchen table. Jordan accepted their hospitality as a chance to calm his nerves before returning to the station. He'd never drawn his gun in a crisis before, leaving him a little shaken.

Jeannie asked, "What the hell was all that about? And who was that poor girl everyone wants so badly?"

Jordan explained about Joanna's murder. "But we still don't know what they're trying to cover up. I hope Samantha can tell us. Hoffman and Lenhart certainly think she knows something."

Ed rubbed the stubble on his chin. "How did you know she was here? We called 9ll, but you got here sooner than the police."

Jordan sipped his coffee. "When we got into Key West tonight, we had no idea where they had Samantha. Hoffman has a condo here in town, so we staked it out. The van driver called him on a cell phone after they crashed and told him Samantha had escaped. Lenhart left the condo, and we followed him. We heard the police report of your call on the radio. We were certain it was Samantha, so we came here and made sure we had enough backup."

He stood to leave and shook hands with the Brightons. "Thanks, folks, you helped save that young woman's life."

"One more thing, Detective," Jeannie asked as Jordan stepped onto the front porch. "Was the handsome young man who caught her Samantha's husband?"

"No, that was Jack Stone, a...uh...very special

friend of hers."

"Well, he seemed anxious to get her back."

Jordan thought about the complicated relationship between Jack and Samantha and how hard they seemed to fight their attraction for each other. He shook his head. "Yes, I imagine he still is."

****

When Samantha awoke in the hospital the following day, Jack held her hand, staring down at it. His appearance startled her—rumpled suit, hair looping over his forehead, deep circles under his bloodshot eyes. He obviously hadn't slept in a while. She winced, guilt overwhelming her.

This was all her fault. If only she hadn't overreacted, distrusting Jack immediately, running off like a spoiled child.

His head jerked up when she moved, and he brightened a little. "Sam, thank God. How do you feel?"

Samantha struggled to find her voice in a throat that was parched and dry. "I don't know," she croaked. She looked around the sterile room, her gaze stopping on the IV needle inserted in her right hand. She lifted her left hand to finger the bandage swathing her forehead, then began to explore the one covering the back of her head. She winced again, this time in pain.

Jack grabbed her hand and brought it gently back to the bed. "Better not, Sweetheart; the doctors had to work quite a while to get you cleaned up and stitched up. Let's not bother it, okay?"

His voice was the kind a parent used with a toddler who was busy climbing the stairs. She didn't mind, though. It was sort of soothing, so she nodded off to sleep.

An hour later, the nurse awakened her to take her temperature and blood pressure. Jack was gone.

"Where's Jack, the man who was here earlier?" she mumbled around the thermometer.

"When he knew you were conscious, he left to change clothes and get something to eat. I'm sure he'll be back soon. He was here all night. He didn't want to leave this morning, but the doctor insisted you would be all right until he got back," the nurse rambled cheerfully, then paused as she replaced the blood pressure cuff in the holder on the wall behind the bed.

She continued as she tapped into her tablet, "He certainly seems devoted to you, Miss Morgan. Offhand, I'd say you're a lucky woman."

Samantha didn't feel lucky. She felt stupid and reckless and angry and hurt, but not lucky. If Jack and Jordan hadn't arrived when they had, she'd be as dead as Joanna.

She ran back through the last twenty-four hours in her addled mind, trying to make sense of the jumble. After her flight from Jack's confession, she was knocked out at the slave labor camp and taken who-knew-where and kept there who-knew-how-long, maybe only a few hours, before she ended up in the warehouse and then the van. She shivered at the thought she might have died along with Flannel Guy when they crashed. Then the dash through reeds to the house on the shore. And those nice people who helped her. *What was their name again?* She couldn't remember. But she would have to find out and thank them.

Then Lenhart and Bill. What an animal he was. And Lenhart! He was going to kill her. Or let Bill do it, probably. And finally, Jack and Jordan bursting through the door, manhandling Lenhart, and scaring Bill enough to pitch her like a hot potato to Jack.

Jack saved me. Again.

"Yes, I guess I am lucky," Samantha said.

"You were rescued from a pretty bad situation from the looks of it, and you have the most handsome man in Key West glued to your side. You're lucky, all right."

Samantha's head shot up, and she nailed the nurse in her stare. "Key West? I'm in Key West?"

"Well, yes, didn't you know?"

"No, I had no idea. I knew I was near the ocean. That's all." The realization of what had almost happened gripped her. "Dear God, they were going to murder me in Key West, like they did Joanna." She slumped back onto the pillow, her head throbbing.

****

"I'm afraid I don't remember much after the wreck, Detective Jordan," Samantha apologized to the stocky man sitting beside the bed. Jack stood quietly by the window, watching her. She shifted nervously under his steady gaze.

What was he thinking? Was he angry? Hard to say. His steely expression gave little away. Exhausted? Definitely. Glad his assignment was over? Probably.

She had told them about Lenhart and Hoffman's revelation regarding Joanna's murder, that it had been Lenhart Joanna was dating, and it was he who was snorkeling with her when the animal, Bill, killed her.

"It's not important if you don't remember. A very nice couple helped you, and we were able to get there in time. You've told us all the vital things except one." He paused, his pen suspended over the page in his notepad where he'd been busily jotting notes.

"What's that?" she asked from her place in the bed, propped up on several pillows, feeling a little more human after eating lunch.

"Why was Joanna murdered in the first place? And did you find out what she found out?"

"Yes. I found out that night in the fog when I left the inn," she said, her voice dying away when Jack turned his back to her and stared out the window. She turned to Jordan. "They're running a slave labor camp in the woods outside Meredith, not far from their plant. That's where the bulk of the clothes are made. By North Koreans Hoffman betrayed and imprisoned there."

Jack turned to face her, his eyes glinting like metal in the dim room. "A slave camp? How did you find it?"

Samantha thought she might as well start at the beginning, although she knew it made her look like a fool to take off alone into the woods and follow the truck, especially when the worst that could have happened did.

"I left the inn and went out to the same road we traveled every day to Green Earth. I guess I wasn't thinking clearly, and I let the car take me." She paused. Jack turned back to the window.

Devoted, hah! He thinks I'm an idiot! He won't even look at me. Well, it's his fault I left the inn that night. If he, Jordan, and my father hadn't concocted the whole protection scheme without telling me, none of this would have ever happened. If he hadn't lied to me about...everything. All the things he said, all the things we did, were lies!

Samantha clenched her fist against the bed, then willed herself to continue her story. "The fog got thicker, so I pulled onto the shoulder. I was turning around to come back to town when a truck marked FISH, like the ones from Green Earth, went barreling past. I decided to follow, and it led me to a little trail going to the compound. I tried to call you, but there was no signal. I parked the car and watched them load garments into the truck. I could see the people working in these little, dingy shacks in the middle of the night—children, too. I was coming back to tell you, but the car wouldn't start, and then someone hit me on the head from behind. I blacked out, and when I woke up, I was in a warehouse, apparently here in Key West. You know the rest."

Jordan whistled under his breath when she finished her story. He scribbled furiously on his notepad.

Jack continued to stare out the window, his back arrow straight and rigid as an iron bar. He seemed to Samantha as immovable as a mountain and unreadable as granite.

"I still have a couple of questions for you," she asked Jordan.

"Okay, ask away."

Jack took a step closer to them.

"Who was S.L.? Was that even a thing?"

Jordan answered, "We did a little digging into Lenhart's background. Elgin is his first name. His middle name is Sloan. That's what he went by in school, but when he got older, he used his given name instead. Joanna still knew him as Sloan."

Jack sighed. "Good grief."

Jordan asked Samantha, "Your other question?"

"Who car bombed us in St. Louis?"

Jack answered, "That was Lenhart. Hoffman didn't know he was off the rails and conducting his own operation. That's why Hoffman denied knowing anything about it. Lenhart was also the one behind the threats to the company. He was trying to put Joanna off by scaring her. And then you. He confessed everything."

Samantha fell back against the pillows, closing her eyes. "I'd like to sleep now."

"Of course, we'll talk more later," Jordan said, closing the notepad. He patted her hand, then left, closing the door softly behind him.

She opened her eyes when Jack crossed the room to stand by the bed. His face was a mask of control, his jaw twitching. Samantha was stunned by the power in the man.

"Jack, I…"

He placed his finger on her lips, then bent to kiss her. It was a kiss as full of raw strength and controlled passion as his expression. His lips found hers, softly at first, moving over them, then deeper, the pressure building and building until it abruptly stopped, and he pulled away, breathless.

"I'm sorry, Sam, so sorry."

He turned and left the room.

Samantha closed her eyes again, and a single tear escaped down her cheek.

****

Out in the hall Jack leaned against the wall, inhaling the antiseptic hospital air, clenching and unclenching his fists at his sides, willing his heart to quit its pounding in his chest. He needed to calm down, do something, anything, to regain control of his temper, his anger, his blinding rage at the men who nearly killed Sam.

Seeing her in Bill's arms, struggling, beaten, bruised and bleeding, nearly killed *him* and awakened feelings he didn't know he even possessed. In all his years in the service, in the throes of war, in harrowing firefights, narrow escapes, imprisonment and even torture, he had always been in control of himself. It was how he had survived. But those times had never been about someone he was sworn to protect, someone he cared about, someone he loved.

Standing there in the hallway, leaning against the wall, he knew he would have killed for Sam. To protect her, to save her, to avenge her.

That knowledge scared him. And it told him something important. Something he needed to confide to Sam. If only she would hear him.

After a few moments he pushed away from the wall and went back into her room, where he stood in the doorway, watching her sleep.

The sunset burned through the blinds, casting shadows over the bed, the floor, and her sleeping figure. She seemed small and vulnerable, and Jack wanted nothing more than to take her in his arms and carry her off to a secluded place. Somewhere he could keep her safe and close.

But that wasn't likely to happen now.

The trust between them had been shattered. She no longer believed he loved her. She no longer believed he had come to New Hampshire to be near her. She was convinced that what had happened that night (was it only three nights ago?) was an empty seduction on his part, to keep her from asking too many questions about why he had followed her.

He wanted to explain about that night and how his protecting her was no longer a job. He wanted to share his plans for the future and make her believe he loved her.

He moved to the side of the bed and sat in the chair,

taking her hand in his. He brushed a kiss across her forehead, then fearing it might be his last chance, he stole one from her lips.

She sighed and turned her head to face him. "Jack, you came back."

"Yes, Sweetheart, I've been here a while, watching you sleep."

"Mmm, how fun for you."

"It's not that bad. You're beautiful when you sleep."

She grimaced. "Yes, I look especially lovely now, with this big bandage on my head."

He leaned over and kissed the bandage in question. "Yes, you do."

Her expression darkened suddenly. "I'm sorry I ran off. It was a stupid thing to do."

Anger against Lenhart and Hoffman and his own failure welled up inside him again. "You were nearly killed," he growled.

A blush crept up Samantha's face. "I wouldn't have left if you hadn't betrayed me!"

She misunderstood! He wasn't angry with her. She had every right to be mad. He had to explain. "I didn't betray you. I was trying to protect you. Your father and Jordan…"

"I know, you hatched this big conspiracy to save me. Well, you could have told me, talked to me, confided in me. I'm not a child who has to be kept in the dark."

"I never said you were a child. But we knew you'd refuse protection. You're so damn independent! And look where it got you!" He gestured to the hospital bed.

Sam's furious expression dissolved into hurt and guilt. Tears poured in rivers down her cheeks.

Remorse for letting his emotions get the best of him

overcame him. He put his arms around her, being careful of the tubes and bandages. "I'm sorry, Sam. I didn't mean to upset you. That's the last thing I want to do."

She sniffled against his chest. "What *do* you want, Jack?"

He put his hand under her chin and lifted her face to his. His gaze lingered on her eyes. Like liquid emeralds. What did he want? To take her in his arms and make love to her all night. To build her a house in the country. To give her lots of beautiful children. To create a life together.

But it was too soon. She was wounded, injured, and vulnerable. She needed time to heal. He would use the time to restore her faith in him. To rebuild her confidence in his love.

He kissed her lightly on the cheek, then stood. "I want you to get some sleep."

As he closed the door to the room, he recognized the unmistakable form of R.L. Morgan coming down the hall. Grace hurried to keep up. It struck Jack she was a lovely, older version of Sam.

"Stone!" R.L. bellowed, pumping Jack's hand for all it was worth. "Good to see you, son. Can't thank you enough for watching out for Sam. I know she's grateful."

"I wouldn't exactly call it that, sir."

"Nonsense, why wouldn't she be grateful to you for saving her life?"

"You may need to ask her yourself, sir."

"Well, all right, I will."

Grace hugged Jack. "Even if my daughter isn't grateful to you, I certainly am." She kissed his cheek.

Jack caught the faintest whiff of the same perfume Sam wore. His heart twisted in his chest. "You're welcome, Mrs. Morgan. I'm glad she's safe. If you'll excuse me, I have a plane to catch."

Mrs. Morgan raised one eyebrow. "You're not staying until Samantha can leave the hospital?"

"No, now you're here, she'll be in good hands. I think the doctor is letting her go tomorrow anyway."

"She'll be disappointed you've left."

"I doubt that."

The older woman stared at Jack for a long moment. He shifted from one foot to the other, uncomfortable under her gaze. Grace Morgan's stare unnerved him, as if her brilliant green eyes could bore a hole through him.

Jack was saved by R.L., who interrupted, "I guess we'll be seeing you in Dallas, then."

"Not for a while, sir, my assignment here is finished. However, after I take care of business out of town, I'd like to talk to you."

"Of course, of course, any time. Did you want to discuss something in particular?"

"Well, I'm still formulating the plans. I'll explain when I come back to Dallas."

Grace brightened. "So, you'll be coming back to Dallas?"

"I certainly hope so."

Grace smiled at him. "I hope so, too."

Unaware of the surreptitious glances between Jack and Grace, Morgan said, "All right, then, let my secretary know when to expect you."

"Thank you, sir. I'll see you then. Goodbye, Mrs. Morgan."

He strode down the hall, feeling the heat of Grace's stare penetrating deep into his soul.

****

218

"Mother! Daddy!" Samantha cried out as her parents came into the room. Her father took one look at her and remained immobile by the door, his face pale. Her mother flew to the bed and hugged her quickly, then inspected the bandages swathing Samantha's head.

"I'm fine. Both of you, calm down. Daddy, come here and sit by me." She patted the bed and gave her father the most reassuring smile she could muster.

Her mother perched on the edge of the chair, holding Samantha's hand. "Detective Jordan called us early this morning, and we were frantic to get here. We had a terrible time getting a flight out. Everything was booked."

"I'm glad you're here." Samantha squeezed her mother's hand. "I'm sorry you were worried."

She glanced at her father, who looked a little queasy. "Daddy, are you all right?"

He waved her concerns away. "Of course. It's a shock seeing you like this. Where's the doctor? I'd like to have a word with him."

"Her, Daddy. Dr. Matheson is a woman. But she's gone for the day. You can speak to her tomorrow."

"Well, what has she told you?"

"She put a couple of stitches in each cut, and she says I'll have a few teeny scars, but nothing serious. I had a concussion, but I should be fine."

Her mom shook her head. "Good heavens, Sam, you could have been killed. Thank God Jack and Detective Jordan were there."

Samantha turned to her father. "I wanted to talk to you about that very thing, Daddy. I don't appreciate you hiring Jack to follow me around like a guard dog. I am perfectly capable of taking care of myself."

Her dad guffawed, "Not from where I sit, young lady."

Samantha blushed, thinking how she must look in bed, bruised and battered, with her head wrapped in gauze—not exactly the picture of self-reliance. "Never mind that. You know how I feel about you interfering in my life, Dad. You have to accept I'm grown now and on my own." She paused and considered her next statement carefully. "In fact, the interference of the three of you caused all this trouble. If you had told me the truth initially, I might not have liked it, but Jack and I could have worked together."

"What do you mean, Sam?" her mom asked.

"Well, Jack wove a pretty complicated web of lies to convince me his trip to New Hampshire was his own idea. When I found out otherwise, I left the inn." She lowered her head at the memory of Jack and their confrontation at the inn. "That's when I discovered Hoffman's slave camp, and they discovered me."

Her mom shuddered. "Detective Jordan told us all about it. How awful. Holding all those poor people prisoner!"

Her father looked at her mother, his eyes full of warmth, then explained to Samantha. "He told us on the phone the New Hampshire authorities have been notified, and the people have been found."

"What will become of them?" Samantha asked.

"I don't know, honey. They came into the country illegally, but there were mitigating circumstances. We'll have to see."

Her mom studied Samantha for a few minutes, then said, "We met Jack in the hall."

"He seemed to think you didn't want to see him."

Samantha's head shot up. "Why do you say that?"

Her mother answered, "He said so—right before he left."

"Left the hospital?"

"No, left Key West."

Chapter Fourteen

"I'm sorry, Miss Morgan, Mr. Stone is out of town. Would you like his voicemail?" The secretary at Bolton Valor sounded chipper, which only irritated Samantha further.

"No, thank you. When do you expect him?"

"I'm not sure."

"Is he on an assignment?"

"I'm sorry, I'm not at liberty to say."

"Of course, thank you." She hung up and stared at the phone in exasperation.

She'd been back in Dallas for two weeks, at work for one, and still had not heard a word from Jack. Her brow furrowed, which hurt the cut on her forehead. The bandages were gone, but she still had an ugly red gash the doctor said would heal nicely, with little scarring. Though sore, the wound on the back of her head was less noticeable since her thick hair covered it.

Bobbie had driven her crazy trying to take care of her since she returned to work, bringing her coffee and sweet rolls, screening all her calls, and ordering in lunch. She had finally had enough and snapped at the poor thing that morning.

Guilt-ridden, Samantha called her over the wall that separated their offices, "Bobbie, would you come here for a second?"

In an instant, the older woman appeared at the

doorway, notepad in hand

"Sit down. I want to apologize for being short with you this morning. I've been on edge since I got back. I didn't mean to take it out on you."

Tears threatened to spill from Bobbie's brown eyes. "That's all right, Miss Morgan. I'm so glad you're back and you're safe. I shudder to think what happened to Miss Levinson might have happened to you. I don't think I could have stood it. Losing both of you that way." She began to sob in earnest. Samantha got up and went around the desk, putting her hand on the woman's shoulder.

"I know. I'm sorry I wasn't more aware of how hard it must have been for you."

"I was so worried when I heard you'd been hurt. It was so different from the news I was expecting," Bobbie sniffled, and her voice trailed off when she caught the puzzled look on Samantha's face.

"What news were you expecting?"

"Oh, nothing. Mr. Stone said…"

"Jack, what did Jack say?"

"He didn't say anything concrete. But I thought he meant…" Bobbie squirmed in her chair.

"What? Meant what?"

"Oh, Miss Morgan. When Mr. Stone said he was going to New Hampshire to surprise you. I thought he was planning to ask you to marry him. I even said so, and he didn't deny it. He made me promise to keep it quiet."

"Ask me to marry him?"

"Yes, I tried to keep it quiet, but you know how it is. I was so excited; it might have slipped out to a few people."

"That must be why everyone keeps nudging each

other whenever they see me. I thought it was this stupid cut on my head."

"No, we're all waiting for the announcement." She smiled up at Samantha, her expression full of hope. "Is there going to be an announcement, Miss Morgan? Are you and Mr. Stone engaged?"

Samantha returned to her seat behind the desk and smoothed out the wrinkles in her skirt. "No, Bobbie, there's not going to be an announcement. We need to put this whole incident behind us and get back to business as usual."

"Yes, Miss Morgan. Business as usual." She closed the unused notepad, stood, and left the room, her face clouded over in sadness.

Samantha tried to work, opening the mail and reading one piece over and over. She finally set it aside and stared at the black computer screen.

He was going to ask me to marry him? He never hinted he was serious about our relationship. Oh, sure, he told me he loved me that night in bed, but that was just the heat of passion. I'm sure he didn't mean it, did he? Could he love me enough to want to marry me? Or was that an excuse to get Bobbie to tell him where I was?

And where was Jack, anyway? He had never called or come to see her after leaving the hospital. He certainly wasn't acting like someone who loved her and wanted to marry her. Apparently, that feeling had vanished into thin air somewhere between Key West and Colorado. And there was no point in searching for it anymore.

Only Jack had been able to open her heart to the possibility of true love. She had locked it up tightly after Gary's lies. She had given up on her dreams of a big house full of children, sharing it with a man she adored and trusted. A man like Jack.

No, not like Jack, Samantha thought, as she turned the key on the lock that made her heart a prisoner once again.

****

Turk shook his proud head and pranced sideways.

"He's showing off for you." Steed laughed, watching the groom struggling to control the spirited horse. "Are you sure you want to ride him again? I can have Eddie saddle Lady Lucy. She's a little less rambunctious."

"Oh, no. Turk and I go way back. I've been looking forward to this." Samantha eyed the big roan warily, took a confident step forward, put her booted foot in the saddle, and swung herself up. Turk stepped backward, then stopped stock still when Samantha commanded, "Whoa!"

She raised one eyebrow and nodded at Steed. "I guess we're ready, Mr. Lambert."

He seemed highly amused by the whole scene. "Then let's ride, Miss Morgan."

She and Steed trotted out of the paddock and down the gentle slope behind the barn, skirting the field of windmills. Despite the tremor of fear running through her at the sight of them, Samantha was still struck by the eerie beauty of the shiny silver monoliths, spinning silently.

Steed broke into her reverie. "Did you hear we caught the poacher who shot at you?"

Samantha was stunned. "You mean it *was* a poacher?"

"Yes, we found him a couple of weeks ago, traipsing through the woods, carrying several rabbits. The bullets from his gun matched some we found by the tree. He told us what happened in exchange for a lighter sentence."

"What *did* happen?"

"Well, he was walking with his loaded rifle along the edge of the woods next to the windmills. He tripped over an exposed root, and the gun discharged when he fell. Apparently, he never even saw you until he got up and heard you screaming. He high-tailed it off the property when he realized what he'd done. But of course, he wasn't frightened enough to stay away for long."

"So, it wasn't an attempt on my life?"

"No, guess not." He looked quizzically at Samantha. "You look disappointed."

She laughed. "Not disappointed at all. It's ironic. If I hadn't thought someone shot at me that day, things might have turned out very different indeed." She shook her head.

Samantha knew there was one unanswered question in her desire to wrap up the loose ends from her visits to the ranch. "Steed, there is one thing I'd like to know." She was embarrassed to ask, but the need to know kept gnawing at her. She pressed on. "When I was here that first day, you got a phone call that seemed to really upset you. I couldn't help but overhear. It sounded like someone trying to back out of a deal. And you weren't having any of it."

Steed's brow furrowed in thought. Then he threw back his head and laughed. "That was Marcos, my golfing buddy. One night he had a little too much to drink and challenged me to a competition, swearing he could beat me by four strokes on eighteen holes the next week. The wager was a case of really good malt liquor." He chuckled.

Samantha grinned. Clearly Steed enjoyed this story.

"So, when he sobered up, he realized there was no way he could beat me by that much, if at all. He wanted to renege on the deal. So, I teased him about it. I'm kind of surprised I sounded threatening."

Samantha laughed, too. "You were pretty convincing."

"Maybe I should be an actor."

She shook her head. "No, you're much better doing what you do. But did Marcos lose and pay up?"

"Yeah, but I let him off the hook for just one bottle of whiskey and a steak dinner."

So, it was a poacher, after all, and a good-natured rivalry between friends. Nothing the least bit suspicious. Samantha chided herself for mistrusting such a gentle, generous man.

She and Steed rode companionably for an hour, then stopped at the same place they had been on their previous ride: under the pecan trees. The ground was carpeted in autumn-hued leaves.

Samantha adjusted Turk's bridle as a flurry of leaves fluttered around her. She turned to see Steed looking pleased with himself. She never failed to be impressed by how thoroughly Texan he was, his hands on his slim, blue-jeaned hips and the collar of his denim jacket turned up against the brisk November day. The ever-present Stetson pulled over his blue eyes didn't hide the mischief dancing there.

She stepped behind Turk, grabbed a handful of leaves, and hurled them at Steed. They floated harmlessly to the ground several feet in front of him.

"Oh, you'll have to do better than that, Samantha," he teased, wafting a barrage at her.

"Those are fightin' words, Steed Lambert," she said, scooping up an armload of leaves, stalking the ten feet separating them, and tossing them into his grinning face.

"You've done it now!" He challenged and came after her, his fists full. She screamed and ran around the nearest tree, hiding behind it.

Steed followed, chasing her back to the horses and tackling her in a pile of leaves at the base of a spreading pecan tree. She landed on her back. Steed landed on top of her.

They both laughed breathlessly. Then Steed stopped laughing and kissed her. His mouth found hers open and receptive, still laughing. She welcomed his lips against hers, the warmth of his body pressed close, his arms wrapped firmly around her, cradling her head. It had been weeks since New Hampshire, weeks since Jack. She needed to know she could still be wanted by a man, still *want* to be wanted.

She responded to Steed's kiss, looping her arms around his neck, knocking off his hat, and running her fingers through his sandy hair. The kiss deepened. He held her closer to him and searched the depths of her mouth, leaving her gasping.

"Sweetheart," he whispered against her ear as his hands roamed over her back, kneading the skin beneath her sweater.

Samantha heard Steed's voice, but that was what Jack called her. Her eyes flew open. Steed wasn't Jack. His hands weren't Jack's hands. His lips weren't Jack's lips. It wasn't Steed who conjured up this response in her body. It was Jack. It was Jack she wanted. It was Jack she wanted to *want her*.

"Steed, no," she mumbled, pushing firmly against

his chest. "I can't do this." She scrambled to her knees, tumbling him to his back. He stared up at her, bewildered.

"I'm sorry, I can't do this," she repeated. "I like you very much. And it wouldn't be fair to you."

"Stone," he muttered, pulling his hat back down over his forehead and clambering to get to his feet.

Samantha ignored him. "Let's ride back, okay?" She mounted Turk and waited while Steed swung into the saddle of his night-black horse.

They rode in silence until they reached the barn, turning the horses over to the groom. Steed walked her to the car, then leaned into the window.

"I'm sorry, Samantha, I didn't realize you and Stone were still involved."

Miserable, Samantha stared at the steering wheel, refusing to meet his gaze. He hooked his thumb under her chin and gently turned her head to face him. "That's it, isn't it? Lie to me, Samantha. I'd hate to think you rejected me on general principle."

She smiled. "It isn't you. Or general principle. You're a wonderful man, Steed, and I'm sure I'm the biggest fool who ever lived."

He kissed her forehead. "*He's* the luckiest *guy* who ever lived." Then Steed backed away from the car and waved as she drove through the Eco-Tek gate and onto the road.

****

"So, who's the orphan this year?" Samantha asked, tasting a morsel of the cornbread dressing.

"That's not a very nice thing to say about the person your father has invited for Thanksgiving," Her mother chided Samantha as she chopped onions for giblet gravy.

"Sorry, Mom, ever since I was little, I've always thought of the people Daddy invited on Thanksgiving as orphans. Now, I know they usually had family, but couldn't get home for the holidays. It's one of the things about Daddy I love. He's very soft-hearted, you know."

"Well, of course, I know he's soft-hearted, Sam," her mom said, swooshing a stray hair out of her eyes with the back of her hand. "Here, cut the celery."

She handed Samantha several stalks.

"So, who is it this year?" Samantha persisted. She took a knife from the butcher block on the counter and chopped the celery into pieces.

"Oh, I don't know, someone we haven't had before, I think," her mom answered vaguely, then wiped her hands on the apron around her waist. "I need to check the table. Keep chopping. Do apples after that for the fruit salad." She hurried into the dining room.

Samantha and her mother had prepared Thanksgiving dinner much the same way for the last twenty-five years. Samantha remembered standing on a chair, mixing the ingredients for one thing or another, then graduating to setting the table, stirring the gravy, and now helping equally in the holiday ritual.

She and her mom had awakened early to roast the turkey, then leisurely moved into preparation of the traditional Morgan family feast. Since the family was small, and Samantha was the only child, R.L. had always brought home an "orphan" from the office to share in their family's bounty.

Samantha never minded. It was nice having more people around on the holidays. She had always regretted not having lots of brothers and sisters running around. So, she looked forward to sharing the meal with someone who might be missing their own family on that special day.

When she finished the fruit salad, she put the bowl in the refrigerator to chill, untied her apron, and surveyed the kitchen. *Not too big a mess. I'll load these things into the dishwasher, baste the turkey again, and run upstairs to dress.*

The doorbell rang as she ascended the back staircase to her childhood room on the second floor. She closed the door and muffled the sounds of voices drifting up the front stairs.

Samantha had worn jeans and an old University of Texas sweatshirt in the kitchen, so now she slipped into the clothes she had brought from her apartment—a purple velvet tunic, black leggings, and little booties. It was comfortable—she and her mother would be up and down a lot serving dinner—but she had always thought purple was a flattering color with her green eyes. As she studied her reflection in the mirror, she noticed the scar on her forehead had diminished, and she looked healthy, if not entirely happy.

She practiced smiling, and the expression captured her mouth, cheeks, and even her hair as she tossed it gaily. But the smile never reached her eyes. They were still green, but the light had left them. Even Samantha could tell. She shook her head at the sad-eyed woman in the mirror, hastily applied lipstick and blush, then scurried downstairs to see who their Thanksgiving "orphan" might be.

****

It was impossible not to recognize the broad shoulders, barely contained in the well-tailored sports coat, the wavy black hair, and the rumbling laugh filling the room with warmth.

God help me, it's Jack.

"Jack." Samantha breathed his name from the living room doorway. He had his back to her, he and her father talking animatedly in front of the fireplace.

He turned around to face her, and she was struck again by the man's powerful presence, sleek good looks, and catlike grace.

Pulling herself together with some difficulty, Samantha crossed the room and extended her hand to Jack in a courteous, if formal, greeting. "Jack, so you're our orphan this year."

His face immediately clouded over, and Samantha regretted her unfortunate choice of words. "I'm sorry, that was clumsy of me. I wasn't thinking," she murmured, hoping he would forgive her.

Her father jumped into the awkward silence. "That's what Samantha always calls the folks I invite to Thanksgiving." He laughed and pounded Jack on the back. "Not that any of them are actual orphans, only at the holidays."

Samantha shot Jack a pleading look. He smiled, and she was surprised to find his expression wasn't as angry as she expected. Instead, barely disguised passion darkened his gray eyes.

"Yes, sir," he said. "I can't seem to get home." Jack continued carrying on a conversation with her father. about business until her mother appeared at the door.

"Samantha, why don't you take Jack out on the patio and introduce him to Beasley while your father helps me in the kitchen."

Jack cocked his head at Samantha. "Beasley?"

Samantha led him through the sliding glass doors

onto a wide redwood deck surrounding a swimming pool. Big planter boxes filled with marigolds were interspersed among various lounge chairs, wrought iron tables, striped umbrellas, and an oversized barbecue grill.

Jack eyed the latter appreciatively.

"It's for grilling the fatted calf."

"It's big enough."

"Dad loves to barbecue."

Samantha wandered around the pool, calling, "Beasley! Beasley!"

After a moment, a fat tuxedo cat waddled out from under a bush over to Samantha, weaving in and out of her feet and purring loudly. She leaned over and picked him up, burying her face in his thick fur.

Jack, who had followed her, reached out and scratched the big animal behind his ears. The purring grew louder.

Jack chuckled. "So this is Beasley."

"Yeah, he's a glutton. Mother is shameless about feeding him."

She sat next to him on a creaky wooden glider, their legs touching until the cat snuggled between them. The day was brisk—Thanksgiving weather in Texas—and Samantha shivered slightly.

"Jack, why didn't you come back to the hospital?"

He stroked the cat. "I had a few things to take care of."

"In Colorado?"

"Yes, but first I flew to New Hampshire."

"New Hampshire? Whatever for?"

"I wanted to see to the fate of those North Koreans Hoffman held prisoner, among other things."

Samantha was not expecting that. A humanitarian mission from Jack Stone? Did she know so little about this man?

"What did you find out?" she asked, enthralled.

"Well, the Meredith police and the folks from ICE found the camp where you said it was. They rounded up the people and decided how to handle such a terrible situation. They are all desperate for political asylum, and it appears they'll get it once the hearings are complete. The churches in Meredith and several other communities have offered to sponsor them for citizenship. There have also been offers from Korean communities throughout the U.S. to take them in."

Tears stung Samantha's eyes. She remembered the haunted faces of the people she had seen in the camp, trapped and hopeless. "That's wonderful, Jack. I'm so glad. Those people deserve a chance at freedom and happiness after what they've been through."

"You're the one who saved them, Sam." Jack's eyes were full of admiration.

Admiration she didn't deserve. She hung her head. "Jack, I stumbled on them in the middle of doing something stupid. I should never have left the inn, and I should never have followed the truck in the fog. I didn't do anything heroic."

He lifted her chin to meet her watery gaze. "Sweetheart, you kept your head, and you stayed alive. If you hadn't, those people would still be imprisoned. Hoffman and Lenhart wouldn't be awaiting trial. And you'd be dead. I think you're spectacular." He brought her face closer to his. "Now, if I don't kiss you, I'll go crazy."

She didn't stop him as his hungry mouth sought

hers. It was a kiss of passion and fire, deep and long, searing her lips in his flame. He pulled her roughly against him on the swing, holding her so close she thought she might quit breathing.

She fell into him, the heat of his chest, warm against the chill of her skin, the smooth muscles of his arms rendering her powerless to resist if resistance had been on her mind, which it wasn't. She wanted only to sink farther into Jack, lose herself in him, and become one with him.

But apparently that wasn't what he wanted. He had left her to go to New Hampshire. He hadn't spoken to her since Key West. He admired her. Admiration wasn't love. He wanted her; it seemed obvious enough. But did he want her the way she wanted him—for a lifetime?

She pulled herself back to the moment and broke the contact between them, gulping the crisp air. Her lungs burned.

"What's wrong, Sweetheart?" he asked, his thumb caressing her arm.

Her heart lurched at the endearment. "Jack, I…"

A loud, throat-clearing harrumph interrupted her. Her father stood in the doorway. "You two want to come in for dinner? The turkey's ready and waiting."

"We can talk about it later."

Jack stood, determination etched in his face. "Yes, we will."

****

"That was delicious. I'm stuffed." Jack leaned back in his chair, wiping his mouth on the linen napkin.

"He's right, ladies. Scrumptious as usual," R.L. bowed his head toward his wife, then his daughter. "Stone, let's have coffee in the den and turn on the game."

"Well, sir, I'd like to, but I thought Samantha and I might do the dishes. Then Mrs. Morgan could relax for a while." He began gathering dirty plates.

Grace protested, but to no avail. Samantha shooed her parents into the den, promising to bring them coffee and pumpkin pie. She followed Jack into the kitchen, carrying a stack of dishes.

It took a few minutes to clear the table, but when they were in the kitchen, loading the dishwasher, Samantha stopped and put her hands on her hips.

"What's gotten into you, Jack Stone. Do you always do the dishes when you're a dinner guest?"

He felt a little sheepish as he answered. "No, but it seemed like the thing to do since your mother went to so much trouble. I guess it made me feel more like part of the family."

"You are like a part of the family." Samantha didn't tease him anymore.

She carried the coffee and cups on a tray to her parents. Jack followed, balancing plates of pie smothered in dollops of whipped cream.

Grace was clearly uncomfortable at being served by her guest. "Please, Jack, you sit down. Samantha and I will finish."

"Mrs. Morgan, I'd like to finish up, if I may. Besides, Samantha and I have something to discuss."

He whisked her off to the kitchen, steering her through the swinging door.

"What do we have to discuss?" she asked, raising one eyebrow.

"This," Jack answered, grabbing her around the waist and drawing her to him. He kissed her sweetly this time, lingering over her lips as if they were the dessert he longed for. As the kiss deepened, he cradled the back of her head in his hand, lacing his fingers through her hair, moaning softly.

****

The sound broke Samantha's heart. She could no longer stand to be close to Jack and so far away. She wanted all of him. Or she would have nothing at all. She pushed him away and looked into his smoldering eyes.

"Jack, I can't...I can't be with you anymore. You don't love me. What happened between us in New Hampshire was an act. I know that now. I appreciate you were protecting me, but you don't have to pretend anymore. You may even have physical feelings, but that's not enough for me. I want more. I want real love, a home, children, and a life to share with someone. I was foolish to think that someone might be you. After all, why would you settle for a woman as boring as I am when you have your pick of glamorous women all over the world?"

Jack pulled her into a chair at the breakfast table and sat in one opposite. Their knees touched. He took her hands in his, and that familiar electric current shot up her arms.

"Samantha," he began. "I don't want glamorous, empty-headed women. I want a beautiful, exciting, challenging woman. I want you."

She shook her head and began to protest. He silenced her, his finger to her lips.

"Listen to me. What happened in New Hampshire was as real for me as it was for you. And equally surprising. Yes, it's true I went after you under false pretenses, but that lasted five minutes. I discovered I was in love with you. I think I have been since I met you."

Tears sprang into Samantha's eyes. She couldn't believe what she was hearing. "Jack, you told Bobbie you were going to ask me to marry you. You weren't, were you?"

"No, not at first. I had to let her believe I was going to New Hampshire to be near you. We didn't want anyone, especially you, to know I was protecting you." He lifted her hands to his mouth and kissed the palms. "But the truth is I was going to confess the whole thing and ask you to marry me that night after the cruise. But Jordan showed up and ruined everything."

"You were?" Her heart began to pound in her ears.

"Yes, and since that didn't work out, I'm going to ask you now." He slipped out of the chair, pulled a box from his jacket pocket, and then dropped onto one knee in front of her.

"Samantha Morgan, will you marry me?"

Samantha slid out of the chair to her knees beside him. "Oh, Jack! Are you sure?"

He grinned. "Yes, Sweetheart, I've never been more sure of anything."

She twined her arms around his neck and gazed into his soft gray eyes. "I'm sure, too. I love you, Jack."

"I love you, too." He kissed her in the middle of the kitchen floor.

After a few moments, he remembered the box in his hand. "I have something for you. It's the only thing I have of my mother's."

He opened the box to reveal a platinum engagement ring—a single, square-cut diamond flanked by two baguettes. Samantha began to cry as she cradled the velvet box in her hand.

Jack rushed to relieve her. "It's okay if you don't like it. We'll choose something else. Maybe you'd like something gold."

She looked at the man who would be her husband and loved him more than she could fathom. The gift of his mother's ring, so stunning in its simplicity, so perfectly like what she would have chosen, touched her deeply. "Jack, it's the most beautiful ring I've ever seen. I'm honored you want me to have it."

He slipped it on her finger, then kissed each of the others before relinquishing her hand. "Let's go tell your folks." He helped her up from the floor.

****

Samantha thought it odd her parents didn't seem surprised by the news.

Her father gave Jack a great bear hug and pumped his hand enthusiastically. "Welcome to the family, son. Couldn't be happier about this."

Her mother hugged Samantha then Jack. "It's about time. I couldn't imagine how long it would take to get you two together. I was going to keep inviting Jack to dinner until he proposed." Laughing, she turned to her daughter. "Or you did."

Samantha stared at her mother. "You planned this?"

"Of course," she said smugly. "When I watched you sparring in Key West, I said, 'these two belong together.' So, I helped things along a little."

Jack picked her up and swung her around, then set her down and kissed her soundly on the cheek. "Thank you, Mrs. Morgan. You are a wise woman."

Samantha added, "And a sneaky one."

They all sat down in the den, oblivious to the bowl game on television.

Her mother asked, "When will the wedding be?"

"Well, that's the second part of my surprise for Sam," Jack said, mischief dancing in his eyes.

"Second part? What do you mean?" Samantha snuggled closer to him, digging in his jacket pockets. "More lovely jewelry?" She reached into his coat pocket and pulled out a long envelope. "What's this?"

"Well, I was hoping we could get married at Christmas. Then we could use these for the honeymoon."

Samantha held up the envelope. "What are they?"

He turned to Samantha and cupped her face in his hands. "A long time ago, you told me about someone who disappointed you. I don't ever want you to be disappointed again."

Samantha's hand began to tremble as she realized what Jack had done. He took the envelope from her and held her hands to his chest.

"These are plane reservations, Sam. Would you spend Christmas with me, as my wife, in Williamsburg? Your parents are more than welcome to join us."

The tears spilling down Samantha's cheeks were filled with enough joy to last a lifetime of Christmases. Here, at last, was a man who understood her, a man she could trust, a man who would give her the things she longed for.

****

"Quit yelling, Vince!" Jack said, raising his voice to be heard over his boss' angry tirade.

He had returned to Winding Creek, Colorado to meet Vince at Bolton's Valor Security and Investigations headquarters. There were things that needed to be said, and they needed to be said in person. But Vince, who paced around the office like a caged lion, wasn't letting him get a word in edgewise.

"You did exactly what I told you not to do. You got involved with that woman in Dallas! Her mother has called here a dozen times demanding I send you back. *Her mother, Jack!* Then after Thanksgiving things went radio silent. What the hell happened?"

"That's what I want to talk to you about. If you'll sit down."

Growling under his breath, Vince sat behind his oversized glass and chrome desk.

Jack sat across the desk, leaning forward as he spoke. "Look, I got close to Samantha, I admit it. I had to in order to protect her. I managed to keep things platonic until we got to New Hampshire, and I knew neither of us was happy with that arrangement. It was mutual, I assure you."

Vince rolled his eyes. "It always is."

Jack ran a hand through his hair to steady his nerves, then plowed ahead, "Then, when she was kidnapped, something snapped in me. I had to save her. Not because it was my job, but because, for the first time ever, I actually cared about someone." He paused. "And someone cared about me. That hasn't happened since David Thornton took a chance on me, gave me a job, and saved me from a life on the streets."

Vince sat back in his chair, fingers tented in front of him, staring at Jack.

So, he kept going, fueled mainly by the need to get it done. "And now I've asked her to marry me. We love each other, and all I want to do is keep her safe and happy for the rest of her life."

"What are you telling me, Jack?"

Jack took a deep breath. "I'm telling you I quit,

Vince. I can't risk my life protecting other people. Soon, I will have a wife and, hopefully, a family to provide for. I need to be safe, too. I have loved working for you and Jacy. But, I quit, happily, gladly, ecstatically, quit."

He stood and grinned at his boss, who came around the desk and embraced him in a fierce bear hug.

"Thank God," Vince said, laughing. "Because I was going to have to fire you."

Epilogue

The soft morning light striped the bedroom of the old New Hampshire farmhouse, casting odd shadows on the antiques hugging the walls. Two fat cats were curled in fluffy balls at the foot of the bed, which was warmed by handmade comforters.

Samantha gazed at her husband's face. He had fallen asleep after their early morning lovemaking, and the contented expression on his nearly perfect features warmed her heart. After six months of marriage, she was still discovering new and wonderful things about him.

He liked to read before he went to bed. He made cinnamon rolls on Sunday morning. He sang in the shower—on key. And he constantly surprised her.

She kissed his stubbly cheek, then quietly slipped out of bed. She needed to get moving. It was going to be a big day.

"Oh, don't leave me," Jack moaned softly.

"Honey, we have to get up." But she couldn't resist his inviting arms and snuggled back into bed beside him. "They're pouring the foundation for the dining hall today, remember?"

He wrapped his arms around her and nuzzled her neck. "Can't they do it without us?"

"I'm sure they can, but you've wanted to be there for every nut and bolt. I doubt you want them to pour concrete without your supervision."

"Okay, okay. But you taste—mmm—so good." He nibbled on her neck, her throat, the swell of her breasts above the lace bodice of her nightgown.

"Jack, the concrete…" she whispered, her breath ruffling his hair.

He smiled at her, eyes sparkling. "I told them not to start until we arrived." Then, he took possession of her mouth with a devouring kiss.

****

The sun was midway up the eastern sky when Samantha and Jack turned onto the trail leading to the compound where Hoffman had kept the North Koreans as his slaves. A big sign reading "Future Home of the David Thornton Camp" marked the entrance.

Jack led her down the trail to the clearing where Samantha had first seen the prisoners loading garments onto the Green Earth trucks. The scene was very different on this Friday morning in June.

The tower and barbed-wire-topped fence were gone. Dozens of construction workers made various repairs and renovations to the little buildings. A cement truck waited to pour the foundation for a big lodge and dining hall.

Jack, Samantha, and the crew's foreman spread the plans out on the hood of a truck and studied them for the hundredth time.

"So, get the foundation done for the lodge. Then next week, we can start on the pool," Jack said. "We want to get as much done over the summer as possible."

The foreman nodded, then strode off, signaling his men to start work on the concrete.

Samantha looped her arm through Jack's. "Oh, Jack, it's coming together so well! I can't wait until next summer when children are here swimming, hiking, riding…"

"Yeah, it's quite a change for a place that held so much sorrow…" Jack kissed the top of his wife's head. "And danger."

"That's all behind us now. Hoffman and Lenhart are in prison where they belong." Samantha hugged him. Then she chuckled. "I bet Hoffman hated losing Green Earth, especially to Dad."

Jack smiled. "Well, he won't need the company anymore, considering how long he will be locked up. And your dad took particular pleasure in buying it out from under him."

"Now that the negotiations are through, we'll start working there pretty soon. Dad said probably in July."

Jack gazed at Samantha. A faraway look darkened his eyes. "A year ago, I never would have dreamed I'd be here next to you, about to start running a plant that makes clothes out of recycled water bottles."

"And by next summer, this place will be full of screaming foster kids escaping the city for a month in the woods of New England. Thanks to you and your soft heart!" She kissed Jack's cheek.

"Thanks to David," Jack said, smiling. "It's time I did something to repay him for saving my life."

"He would be very proud of you," Samantha said, tears watering her vision. "As I am."

Jack put his arm around her, and they walked over to watch as the foundation was poured for a new life together.

A word about the author…

Cindy Causey taught herself to type in the 8th grade because she couldn't write in her diary fast enough in longhand. A 20-year career as a copy chief and marketing manager at JCPenney followed. Cindy retired in 2007, and started a multi-media production company, Dallas Media Center, with her husband, Scott.

After her first book, a non-fiction work called Cherish the Gift: a Congregational Guide to Earth Stewardship, was published, Cindy began writing fiction. She found her voice in romance, stories of the struggles two people endure on the road to happily ever-after.

Her first two books, A Different Drum and A Hot Time in Texas, were published in 2009 by The Wild Rose Press. Cindy's latest women's fiction, Sensible Shoes, also with The Wild Rose Press, was released in early 2025.

Scott passed away in 2019, and Cindy retired from the media business a few years later. She has continued writing and loves creating characters her readers can identify with. In addition to writing, she enjoys photography, traveling, and spending time with her five grown children and four grandchildren. She would like to see the edges of the entire world from the deck of a cruise ship.

You can read more from Cindy on her blog TheWidowWoman.com or website www.cindycausey.com

Thank you for purchasing
this publication of The Wild Rose Press, Inc.

For questions or more information
contact us at
info@thewildrosepress.com.

The Wild Rose Press, Inc.
www.thewildrosepress.com